GRAYSON

A CHRISTIAN ROMANTIC SUSPENSE

OATH OF HONOR

LAURA SCOTT

READSCAPE PUBLISHING, LLC

Dr. Eve Shaw inwardly sighed as she pulled into the physician parking lot of the Milwaukee College of Medicine located on the same campus as Trinity Medical Center. How embarrassing to be running late to her own presentation. It wasn't Eve's fault—a harried mother of three had rear-ended her near the day care center. The damage to Eve's SUV wasn't bad, the car was drivable, but the young mother had insisted on calling the police to get the accident on record for her insurance company. Why, Eve wasn't sure as most rear-end accidents were the second driver's fault. Maybe she feared Eve would come back at her for some reason. A ridiculous notion as she didn't have time for that nonsense.

On a positive note, her presentation was via a live-streaming platform with other molecular cellular researchers, so at least she didn't have to worry about walking in late to a huge auditorium full of medical students and professors waiting for her. She'd already done her grand rounds presentation to them last month. This was a smaller group of professors who would hopefully be understanding about her tardiness. She pushed out of her driver's side door, grabbed her oversized shoulder bag, and squinted against the bright June sun.

As she strode quickly to the Milwaukee College of Medicine's research institute where her office was located, she glanced at her watch. Her presentation was supposed to start right now. She inwardly winced. By the time she got into her office and booted up her computer, she'd be at least seven minutes la—

Boom! A large explosion rocked the earth beneath her feet. Despite her comfy shoes, she was knocked over, her backside hitting the concrete hard enough to make her teeth rattle. Dazed, she looked up at the research building.

Flames and a long plume of black smoke trailed out of one of the office windows. She blinked, trying to comprehend what had happened.

A gas leak? Had to be. Then she realized the smoke and flames were coming from her office window. Wait. Was that right? She double-checked to be sure, counting the windows. She'd been recently promoted to full professor, which had resulted in a move to a large corner office on the third floor.

There was no mistake. It was her office.

"Ma'am, are you okay?" A uniformed officer rushed toward her from a nearby squad, his expression concerned as other first responders ran toward the research building. She stared up at him in confusion, struck off balance for the second time that day.

"Grayson?" Her voice came out in a high squeak.

"Eve? Are you okay?" Grayson Clark loomed over her. Was she imagining things? She hadn't seen the overwhelmingly handsome and charismatic guy since high school. They had been lab partners in advanced chemistry. And while they'd both graduated in the same class, he was two years older than her because she'd graduated from high school at sixteen.

"Yes." She had no clue Grayson had become a cop. "What happened?"

"I'm not sure." He held out his hand, and she allowed him to help her stand. She was annoyed at the tingle of awareness that raced along her nerves. Then she told herself it wasn't him but the shock over what had transpired. "I was leaving Trinity Medical Center after dropping off a prisoner patient when I saw the explosion."

Shading her eyes with her hand, she looked up at the damaged corner of the building. "That's my office."

"What?" Grayson grasped her arm. "You work in there?"

"Yes, of course." His gaze belatedly dropped to her Milwaukee College of Medicine name badge clipped to her collar. "I'm supposed to be doing a presentation from my office."

Grayson's expression turned grave. "You're saying the bomb was meant for you?"

Her eyes widened as the realization sank deep. "I—well, that seems a bit paranoid, doesn't it? I'm sure it was random, right? I mean, who would want to hurt me?"

"I was hoping you would have that answer." Grayson's dark-brown eyes bored into hers. "I see you're a doctor. Is this related to a patient situation? Or something else?"

"I'm not that kind of doctor." She flushed and ran her fingers through her brown hair. It was a nervous habit she'd thought she'd kicked. "I have a PhD in molecular biology." When he frowned, she added, "I'm a research scientist. I've been working for the past five years on a way to rejuvenate pancreatic cells to essentially cure diabetes."

A horrible thought struck. "My notes! They're inside my office!"

She tried to pull out of his grasp, but he brought both of his hands up to cup her shoulders. "I'm sorry, Eve, but you can't go in there. Don't you have your notes backed up on a computer system?"

A wave of anguish hit hard. She did have most of her notes on the computer, but not all of them. She doodled when ideas came to her and had many notes lying about on her desk and some she'd stuffed in a file folder.

As she stood there, watching the fire burn in her office, she reminded herself that most of her research was still intact. Whatever ideas she'd jotted down on random sticky notes would come to her again.

Wouldn't they? They'd have to.

She was so close to a breakthrough. She couldn't allow a horrible bomb to set her back.

"Dispatch, this is unit eight. I'm at the scene of an explosion at the Milwaukee College of Medicine. Please send additional units to this location."

Realizing Grayson was right about her inability to go inside, she fished in her large bag for her phone. At the very least, she needed to contact Professor Firestein that she wasn't going to make her presentation.

On cue, her phone rang. She pulled it free, and quickly answered, "This is Dr. Shaw."

"You're late," Firestein said irritably.

"I know. There was an explosion in my office." Saying the words was surreal. "I'm afraid we'll have to reschedule."

"Explosion?" Firestein's tone rose in alarm. "What in the world is going on over there?"

That was a really good question. Too bad she didn't have an equally satisfactory answer. "I don't know. Might be one of those groups who assume all researchers use stem cells or animals to get their results." She didn't use either for her field of study, but it was the only theory she could come up with. "I'm sorry for the inconvenience."

"Oh—ah, don't worry about that." He sounded apologetic now. "I'm just glad you're okay. I'm sure you're right about one of those extremist groups. People have no idea what goes into research like ours. But you can guarantee that if they were struck by illness, cancer, or diabetes, or Alzheimer's, they'd be first in line for the new treatments people like you and I have created for them. I hope the police will do a thorough investigation."

"The police are here, and I'm sure they will. I'll be in touch about rescheduling my presentation for another time." She ended the call, unwilling to discuss the issue further. Dave Firestein was a colleague, but the last thing she needed was for him to tell others about this potential setback. Sometimes researchers could be weirdly competitive about getting their research published in top-notch journals. And her cutting-edge research had many of her colleagues impressed and maybe even a little jealous of her success. Especially since she was the youngest professor on staff.

The shrill sound of fire truck sirens split the air. Grayson still held her arm, and now he nudged her back from the burning building.

"I . . . don't know what to do." She hadn't felt this discombobulated since she'd entered college at sixteen. That first year had been difficult. After conquering the world of academia, she'd found her place here within the Milwaukee College of Medicine Research Institute. She loved nothing more than working in her lab.

How much damage had the lab sustained? Would the

equipment be salvageable? She tried not to dwell on the negative, but it wasn't easy. Years of work would be impacted by this explosion. *Years!*

"Tell me again about this presentation of yours." Grayson stepped in front of her, blocking her view of the fire.

She frowned. Hadn't she already done that? Maybe he hadn't heard her clearly because of the fire truck sirens and commotion going on around them. "I'm a molecular biologist. I received a national research grant to fund my project to rejuvenate pancreatic cells in children and young adults to cure diabetes." She waved a hand at the building. "That's my office, and it's close to the lab in the center of the building. My work is important, having the potential to change people's lives for the better. But critical enough to justify something like this? That's difficult to comprehend."

"But what about your presentation?" Grayson pressed. "Tell me more about that."

"I was giving an update on my research to a dozen professors across the Midwest via a live-streaming service. I could explain more, but it's rather technical. I was running late because some woman rear-ended me in front of the day care center . . ." Her voice trailed off.

If she hadn't been hit by the mother of three, she would have been sitting in her office, smiling into her computer screen, and introducing herself to her colleagues at the exact moment of the explosion.

Her knees went weak, and she sagged against Grayson's strong frame as the knowledge sank deep. God had been watching over her today. He had sent that poor mother of three directly into her path at the right moment.

This wasn't just about the loss of her research notes.

The bomb had been planted in her office with the intent to kill her.

A COLD CHILL snaked down Grayson's spine. Difficult to believe that anyone would try to take out a research scientist, but that's exactly what had happened.

And if not for the fender bender, his former high school classmate Eve Shaw would be dead.

"Grayson?" At the sound of his name, he glanced over to see his immediate boss, Lieutenant Joe Kingsley, jogging toward him dressed in full tactical gear, the way he was. Joe reported to Captain Rhyland Finnegan, and this type of bombing was exactly the type of case their tactical team would be called in for.

"Hey, Joe." Up until January, Joe had been a fellow officer, often taking the lead on various situations, which had helped him get promoted to the rank of lieutenant. Like Rhy, Joe wasn't much on titles; he just remained focused on getting things done. "You got here fast."

"Rhy is concerned about the bombing." Rhy was their captain and their explosive device expert, and he'd been training Grayson to become more well-versed in the various devices bad guys used to create death and destruction. "He wants you to stay in the loop on this in case there are more devices. He also has several of our team members en route so that we can evacuate this building and the others nearby to search for additional bombs."

That suited him just fine. The idea of more devices being planted made him anxious to get to work. But they'd need to wait for the firefighters to get the blaze under control.

"Joe, this is Dr. Eve Shaw." Grayson made the introductions. "It's too early to say for sure that she's the target, but that's her office on fire up there. And she was supposed to be there doing a presentation at the time of the explosion."

Joe's eyebrows hiked up in surprise. "Dr. Shaw, do you have any idea who would do something like this?"

"No. It's got to be one of those extremist groups, though." Eve looked pale and shaky. She had been the smartest kid in their entire high school, having graduated as his class valedictorian with a higher than 4.8 GPA. Grayson wasn't nearly as smart; he would have failed that chemistry class if Eve hadn't been his partner.

"What kind of extremist group?" Joe asked.

"Eve is a molecular biologist. She's doing research on a way to rejuvenate pancreatic cells in children and young adults with diabetes, although she doesn't use stem cells or other animal testing. Those types of groups might assume she is, though." He had no clue what that sort of work entailed, but he wasn't surprised by her vocation. Eve had confided in him about her mother's struggles with the disease. He had confidence in Eve's ability to find a cure. "Her office is the source of the explosion. She was supposed to be giving a presentation but was running late. It certainly seems as if she was the target here."

Joe whistled. "Okay, then you need to stick to her like glue until we make sure we have found all the devices."

He nodded grimly. "We need to check her vehicle. And her home."

"The bomb was in my office. I was fine at home this morning," Eve protested.

"The device was placed and detonated according to your schedule," he reminded her. "It's entirely possible that after leaving here, the bomber went to your place to plant another device as a backup." He turned to scan their surroundings, wondering if the bomber was here watching or had already left the scene. He narrowed his gaze on the parking lot. "Which car is yours?"

"The bright-blue SUV." Eve still looked dazed by the near miss. And he didn't blame her. Just the thought of her being killed made his stomach churn.

"Stay here with Joe." He gently pushed her toward his boss. "I'll check it out."

"Do you want backup?" Joe asked with a frown.

"No need. This shouldn't take long." On a cold January night eighteen months ago, their tactical team robot Dot had been used to examine a possible explosive device planted in an apartment mailbox. Unfortunately, the device detonated, blowing Dot to pieces. They had a new robot now, Dot version 2.0, named Dottie that was used by Officer Gully Sullivan, their robot expert. But it would take too long for Dottie to get here, and besides, he was fairly certain he was being paranoid over nothing. If there was a device in her car, it would have detonated in the fender bender.

He crossed the parking lot to Eve's bright-blue SUV. He winced at the color that would stand out from a mile away. Taking his time, he carefully examined the vehicle from a safe distance before moving in closer. Hunkering down, he carefully felt along the wheel wells first, then the bumpers. He noticed the long crack in Eve's rear bumper as he made his way around the vehicle.

When that was completed, he stretched out on his back, pulled a retractable slanted mirror from his pack, sort of a larger version of a dental instrument, and used that to examine the undercarriage. It was painstaking work because he didn't want to miss anything important.

But after a solid fifteen minutes, he deemed the car to

be clean and safe to use. With relief, he rose to his feet and headed back to where Eve and Joe waited.

"It's fine." He glanced at Joe. "I think we need to take a few teammates to sweep her house."

Eve scowled. "The research building is a public place where anyone can get inside. I keep my house locked when I'm not there."

"Wait a minute, what do you mean the research building is a public place?" Grayson didn't like the sound of that. "Wouldn't your office and especially the lab itself be locked?"

"Well, yes, that's true." She nodded, then added, "But the main lobby is open to anyone who wants to come in. Mostly medical students or other adjunct faculty who want to chat with one of us. We're a teaching facility as well as performing research. We have a receptionist who will also schedule meetings for us if necessary." Her eyes widened in alarm. "Do you think Barbara is okay? And what about the other researchers? Has anyone been hurt or . . .?" Again, her voice trailed off.

"It's too early to know," Joe said quietly. "All we can do is pray for the best possible outcome."

Grayson knew Joe, Rhy, and many of their teammates were all believers. At first, he'd been annoyed, not liking the way they'd prayed before eating or discussed various aspects of their faith.

But he'd gotten used to it and had begun to wonder if they were onto something.

"I can't stand it," Eve whispered. "I don't know how I'll live with myself if others died because of me."

"Not because of you, Eve," Grayson hastened to assure her. "Because of the man or woman who planted that bomb. You didn't ask for this."

She bit her lip and shook her head. "I know," she managed. "But still, I want to hear about the conditions of Geoff Abbott and Allan Ballard as soon as possible. They're the two assistant professors with offices closest to mine."

"I'll see what I can do," Joe promised.

Grayson nodded at Joe. "They're going to be tied up here for a while. Let's head over to Eve's house. Make sure the place is clear."

"What's the address?" Joe asked.

The two men looked at Eve, who quickly answered, "I live close, maybe ten to fifteen minutes away on Maple Creek Parkway." She rattled off the house number.

"Okay, that sounds good." He turned to Joe. "Do you want to come along?"

"Yeah, hang on, we need more people to get this done." Joe lifted his hand to his radio and spoke into it. "I need two officers who are closest to the Maple Creek Parkway to meet me and Grayson at the following address."

Grayson heard the call on his radio, too, quickly followed by a response. "This is Roscoe. I'm almost at the research institute."

"Jina here, I'm en route too."

"Great. Peel off and meet us at the private residence of Dr. Eve Shaw," Joe directed. "Grayson and I will meet up with you shortly."

"Ten-four," Roscoe drawled. Despite being with the team for almost six months, replacing their murdered teammate, Kyle, Roscoe often spoke with his native Texas accent.

"Is this related to the bombing?" Jina asked.

"Affirmative. Details to follow." Joe cut off further communication. "Let's hit the road."

Grayson was glad to be doing something constructive.

"Eve, are you okay to drive? Or do you want to ride with me?"

"I can drive." She still looked pale and shaken, but there was a hint of anger in her stormy gray eyes too.

Oddly, he would have preferred she rode with him. But he forced a nod. "I'll walk you to your car."

She didn't respond but turned and walked back to the bright-blue car. He stayed close, without intruding on her personal space. Obviously, the reality of the situation was still sinking in. Her research, and likely others', would suffer because of this.

The work of a fanatic as Eve had suggested? Or something more sinister?

"Are you married? Divorced? Seeing anyone?" he asked. Then realizing how that sounded, he quickly added, "Is there a possibility this bomb was planted by someone close to you in a gesture of revenge?"

"You seriously think someone would kill me because I broke off a relationship?" She stopped at her car to look at him skeptically.

"Eve, I'm a cop. I've seen all sorts of personal situations go bad." He thought about the recent attempt to kill Pastor Isaiah Washington, and the sex-trafficking ring they'd helped bust up a few months before that. People did horrible things to each other every day. "I know you mentioned fanatic groups who think you're doing research with stem cells or animals, but this could be something personal too."

She stared at him for a long moment, then sighed. "I broke off a relationship with Andrew Thomas two months ago. He's a physician's assistant at Trinity Medical Center." She shrugged. "I'm sure he's moved on to the next woman by now. Monogamy wasn't his strong suit."

"Andrew Thomas," he repeated. "What does a physician's assistant do exactly?"

"He works on the diabetes team. That's how we met." She flushed. "He was really interested in my research, and we started dating. At first it was fun, but I soon realized all he cared about was my work. He—wasn't interested in me as a woman."

Grayson frowned. "That's strange. You're beautiful and smart. Why wouldn't he be interested in you as a woman?"

Her flush deepened, and she turned away to dig in her bag. "You asked. I'm just telling you that I broke things off, and he was disappointed at first, but he got over it." She opened her car door. "See you soon."

He ruminated over that as he jogged to his squad. He drove up and over the curb to head into the parking lot. There was a rear exit they'd use to leave, as the firetrucks and other emergency rescue personnel were blocking the main road.

Andrew Thomas would have to be checked into. Maybe he had been interested in Eve as a woman, but she hadn't realized it. He'd given her plenty of cues he was interested when they were in high school, but she'd rebuffed him, staring at him intensely through those light-gray eyes of hers before moving on to the next chemistry assignment.

Granted, Eve wasn't really his type. But she was cute in a sexy-librarian type of way. Back then, he'd also dated about half the cheerleaders, so it wasn't as if he'd suffered for female attention.

But that was in the past. He had changed his approach to women since then, keeping them at a distance. But Eve didn't know that.

What difference did it make? He was here to investigate an attempted murder. He followed her to her small gray brick house where Joe, Roscoe, and Jina were waiting. Her home was small enough that it shouldn't take too long to clear the place.

He quickly joined his teammates and Eve who was handing Joe her keys.

"Eve, will you please wait in your car?" Grayson asked. "Just to be on the safe side?"

She looked as if she might argue but then spun on her heel and returned to her car. Once she slid in behind the wheel, he turned back to the others. "Let's do this."

The four of them approached the house. Inside, he looked around curiously.

No surprise, Eve's home was clean and neat. As predicted, it didn't take long to clear the main living space. There were only two bedrooms and a full basement. One bedroom was an office, the other her master suite. "I'll take the office," Grayson offered.

"Jina, take the garage, then join me in the basement. Roscoe, clear the master bedroom and bath," Joe said.

He entered the office, noting with amusement that this space was not neat and tidy. Eve had papers everywhere and at least a dozen sticky notes pressed on various surfaces. Thinking of her office at the research institute, he approached the desk first. He pulled the chair out and bent to look underneath.

And froze.

A pipe bomb was strapped beneath the desk.

He quickly used his radio to alert the others. "Device found in the office. Evacuate the area ASAP!" Then he took a deep breath and began to slowly back out of the room, anxious to get out of there before it detonated.

CHAPTER TWO

Someone had tried to kill her.

The words reverberated over and over in Eve's mind. She resisted the urge to cover her ears with her hands as if to drown them out. She had never been involved in something like this, and she could barely comprehend this was truly happening.

Yet the scene was imprinted in her mind. Smoke and flames billowing out of her office window.

Please, Lord Jesus, keep my colleagues safe!

The interior of her vehicle was hot and stuffy, so she opened her window a few inches. She couldn't imagine a bomb would be planted here in her house. Sure, she often worked from home writing her research papers. But the heart of her work was in the lab.

The lab that would be out of commission for a significant period of time.

She closed her eyes and tried not to cry. Tears were useless and wouldn't change anything. It was just that she was so close to a breakthrough. She was confident she'd have something amazing to present at the end of the year.

Now she had no idea how long it would take to reconstruct her lost notes. And to get back into the lab to finish her work.

"Eve!" She opened her eyes in shock when she heard Grayson's shout. "Drive out of here."

Her stomach clenched with fear at the seriously grim expression in his dark eyes. "Why?"

"We found another bomb in your home office. You need to get far away."

"And go where?" Another bomb in her home office? This really was a personal attack. "I can't head to my office."

"Okay, then stay inside the car for a few minutes. The rest of the team and our robot Dottie are on the way."

Dottie? They named their robot? It struck her as absurd, but then she was keenly grateful to hear they would use a robot to help disarm the device rather than sending in a live person.

Like Grayson.

"Okay." She swallowed hard, trying not to look scared to death. "Shouldn't you and the others also be in your cars?"

"We're going to evacuate the neighborhood," Grayson said. "Do you know if anyone here is homebound?"

"No, most of them work. There's one stay-at-home mom with twin boys. She's in the white Cape Cod over there." She gestured toward it.

"Thanks." Grayson quickly jogged off. She watched as the four team members spread out and walked to each of her neighbor's homes. Grayson went to the white house to tell Maribeth to leave. Less than two minutes later, the young mother had her twin boys in her minivan and was driving away.

She was glad to know Maribeth and the boys would be okay. And hopefully the other neighbors would be as well.

What sort of person set a bomb in a nice neighborhood like this? Without caring about the innocent lives that were at risk?

Someone evil. But that realization only added to her confusion over the situation. She didn't know anyone who was this evil.

Did she?

There had been an animal rights group that had gathered outside the research lab a couple of weeks ago, holding up protest signs against using animals in research. In the past, Eve knew some researchers had used rats to explore the impact of new medicines. But even that particular form of study had come to a halt when the researcher who'd used rats had left to take a more lucrative position on the East Coast.

It wasn't easy to explain to the general public how important research was. As Dave had said, nobody cared until they were hit on a personal level with a devastating disease. Then they would be all in on doing whatever research was necessary to receive improved medications or, even better, a cure.

And what would be better than a cure for diabetes? A disease that impacted more than 50 percent of the entire United States population?

More police cars arrived on her street, interrupting her thoughts. She noticed the cops parked their squads sideways on both ends of her street to block traffic from entering and leaving the area.

It was almost like watching a movie. Only these were real people, not actors. Several officers used their radio to communicate, and soon she saw a large, boxy truck arrive.

The squad was moved to allow the truck to enter, coming to a stop just outside her house.

Grayson nodded at the guy who climbed out from behind the wheel. Then he crossed over to open her door. "Come with me, Eve. You can't stay here in the blast zone."

She slid out of the car and stood on shaky legs. With a firm hand on her arm, Grayson led her down the street to where the police cruiser was parked across the road.

"I'd like you to stay behind the cars, okay?" He searched her gaze for a moment. "You'll be safe here."

She nodded, although she wasn't sure that was true. All the police officers had helmets and other padded protective gear on now, covering them from head to toe.

"I have spare gear she can use," a tall blond-haired man with captain bars on his sleeves said. "And if she's the target, one of us needs to stay with her."

She caught the brief hesitation, before Grayson said, "I'll stay, Rhy. No worries."

The man called Rhy rummaged in the trunk of a squad. Moments later, she had a helmet on her head and a thick padded vest covering her white lab coat. She probably looked ridiculous, but no one was laughing.

Especially not her.

After Rhy left, she glanced at Grayson. "How does the robot work?"

"Gully is the master of Dottie's controls. I didn't see a timer on the device, so I believe that was one rigged to go off when you used your computer."

Her eyes widened in horror. "They can do that?"

"Yes." Grayson put his arm around her shoulder. "But don't worry, Gully and Dottie can handle it. The device is pretty basic really. And the fact that there's no timer attached is an added bonus. This should be a piece of cake."

Again, she wasn't convinced, but there was no point in anticipating the worst-case scenario. The neighborhood had been evacuated, and the officers working nearby were well protected.

Still, she silently prayed as a squat robotic device was sent through her front door. She clasped her hands together tightly, holding her breath as the man standing behind a large computer monitor with what appeared to be a giant remote control went to work. She would have liked to see how he manipulated the robot but knew Grayson wouldn't let her that close.

"How long will this take?" she asked.

Grayson shrugged. "Depends. Gully doesn't like to rush things. Dottie is a pricey piece of equipment, and we already lost one robot. Gully won't do anything rash with Dottie."

"You lost a robot in an explosion?" She stared at him. "That's terrible."

"A different case," Grayson said hastily. "That device was behind a locked mailbox, so we had no way of knowing it was on a timer."

She shivered despite the warm June sun beating down on them. Obviously, she knew police officers put their lives on the line for others. But this scene playing out before her only emphasized how dangerous Grayson's job was.

Grayson had women tripping over themselves to date him back in high school, and she was certain that hadn't changed much over the years. He was still devastatingly attractive, and women generally flocked to a man in uniform. Much like the cheerleaders had fallen all over the quarterback of their high school football team.

He wasn't wearing a wedding ring, but many men

didn't. Besides, Grayson's marital status was none of her business.

"Come on, Gully," Grayson muttered under his breath. "You can do this."

She stared at the front door of her house, wondering if the robot, Dottie, would come out holding the device. The minutes ticked by with excruciating slowness. She was about to say something when Gully lifted his hand in a fist.

"He's neutralized the device!" For all his confidence, Grayson sounded relieved. "Stay here. I'll be right back."

"Wait, where are you . . .?" But it was too late. Grayson was already halfway down the street, joining Rhy and Joe near Gully and his computer screen. Then to her horror, Grayson picked up a large black box and headed up the sidewalk to go inside her house.

Alone? They'd let him go inside without backup?

Her heart lodged in her throat as she imagined the bomb detonating because Gully and Dottie had made a mistake.

After another long fifteen minutes, Grayson emerged from the doorway, still carrying the black box. She belatedly realized he'd put the defused bomb inside. He carefully set the box inside the large truck, then backed away, a relieved grin creasing his features.

He'd done it. She leaned against the squad, willing her pulse to slow down. It was over, and even better, no one had gotten hurt.

Except it wasn't over. Not really. Not until they uncovered who had planted and detonated those horrible devices.

And why.

GRAYSON STOOD BACK, waiting for Gully to maneuver Dottie out of Eve's house and back into the bomb truck.

Now that Eve's house had been secured, he wanted to return to the research institute to find out more about what had transpired there. He glanced over to where Eve leaned against the squad, still wearing her protective gear.

The bomber had not only taken out her office at the research institute, but had also placed a second device in her home. This guy knew her schedule and her routine. The bomb hadn't been set beneath her bed or anywhere else, just in her home office.

This was definitely about her research and her work as a molecular biologist.

"Good job." Rhy clapped him on the shoulder.

"Thanks. But you're the one who taught me everything I know," Grayson pointed out.

"True." Rhy grinned, then sobered. "The doc is in danger. We need to find a way to keep her safe until we can get to the bottom of this."

"Yeah, I know." He couldn't help glancing toward Eve. "I need to interview her in more detail. She mentioned a couple of coworkers, a former boyfriend, and extremist groups. But I keep thinking there's more to this than we realize."

"Follow your gut," Rhy said. "You seem to have a rapport with her, so take the lead on this."

"I—well, I wouldn't say we have a rapport, but we did attend the same high school. She graduated at sixteen, so I'm not surprised she's achieved a doctorate degree by now."

"High school?" Rhy grinned again. "I bet you were the most popular kid in your class."

"Only with the girls," Grayson shot back. Because it

was true, even though he didn't act on that attraction anymore. It was still too painful to think about. The rest of the team teased him about why he didn't have a steady girlfriend, and he played along, rather than telling them the truth.

"Well, put that charm of yours to good use on the pretty doc and figure out what we need to know," Rhy said.

"I'll take her to the precinct." Grayson didn't bother to point out that the pretty doc—as Rhy called her—was immune to his charm.

"Maybe you should let her take some personal items to go to a hotel," Rhy suggested. "She can't stay here; this guy has already gotten inside once. He'll no doubt try again."

He didn't like the idea of staying in a hotel with Eve, but Rhy was right about the fact that she couldn't stay here. "Fine. I'll take her to the American Lodge."

"Sounds good." Rhy turned away, then glanced at him over his shoulder. "Call me when you have something to go on."

"Will do." He sighed, then turned to join Eve. He pasted a reassuring smile on his face. "We can get you out of that gear now."

"Okay." She took the helmet off first, running her fingers through her chestnut-brown hair. "Thanks. It's hot. I feel bad that you guys have to wear all this in the heat of summer."

"I'm used to it." He took the items from her and stored them in the back of Rhy's vehicle. "I'm going to take you inside so you can pack a suitcase."

She scowled. "Why? You took the bomb out. I should be able to stay here."

"How did this guy get inside?" He kept his tone calm.

"How should I know?" she countered.

"That's the point, Eve. He knows where you live and where you work. He likely knows you drive a bright-blue SUV that can be seen from a mile away. You can't stay here. So please, pack a bag and come with me."

Her agonized expression spoke volumes, but she silently nodded and walked with him to her front door. Once they were inside, she didn't go straight to the master suite, though. She went into her office.

He followed, watching in surprise as she began gathering her papers and sticky notes together. "What are you doing?"

"I can't leave these here." She shot him a look of exasperation. "This was why he planted the bomb here, right? Because he intended to destroy my research? I need to pack it all together, especially now that I've lost everything in my office."

With a sympathetic wince, he nodded. "Okay. Can I help?"

"No." Her voice was thick as if she were on the verge of tears. "I'll take care of it."

He stepped back, giving her some privacy. He could understand why she was upset. He moved back into the living room and pulled out his phone to call the American Lodge.

"American Lodge, this is Gary," a deep voice answered.

"Hey, it's Grayson Clark with Rhy's tactical team." Gary Campbell was a former firefighter who was injured in the line of duty. He bought the motel and did a decent business there. He also offered police and firefighters a discount on rooms. Truth be told, the tactical team used Gary's services often. "I need a set of connecting rooms."

"I have the two rooms on the second floor that you can

use for a few days," Gary confirmed. "But the motel is booked solid over the weekend."

Today was Tuesday, so they would have the room likely until Friday morning. "I'll take them, thanks."

"You got them," Gary said. "I hope you're not bringing more danger with you, though."

"I'll do my best to make sure we're not followed." Grayson knew Gary's motel had suffered damage in the past, but it had been almost six months since anything had happened there, so he felt better about using it as a hideout. Gary had also installed security cameras last year, which helped.

"I'll hold you to that," Gary joked. "Keys will be waiting for you."

"Thanks. See you soon." He slipped the phone back into his pocket and walked back to the office. To his surprise, Eve had all the paperwork, sticky notes, and the laptop computer itself stashed in her large bag.

"Here, hold this for me." She thrust the bag into his arms. "I'll grab a change of clothes and toiletries."

"Sounds good." The bag weighed a ton, and he wondered how much other stuff she had in there. Knowing Eve, it was all work related.

He admired her passion and dedication to her research. But in looking around her house, he noticed there were only a few personal items. A picture of Eve standing between her parents wearing her doctorate hood and gown. He'd never met her parents, but they appeared older, almost as if they could have been her grandparents.

He didn't remember hearing her talk much about her family. Every time he tried to get to know her on a personal level, she'd turned the conversation back to chemistry. She'd made it her mission to help him understand why they were doing the experiments their teacher assigned and what results they were looking for.

After the first week of school, Grayson had considered dropping the advanced chemistry class. But then he'd been partnered with Eve Shaw, the smartest kid in the entire school. So he'd decided to stick it out. It didn't hurt that she was cute and funny. Along with being smart.

"I'm ready." Eve's voice interrupted his trip down memory lane.

"Great." He reached for the handle of the small suitcase she was rolling behind her. "I'll take that."

"Thank you." She glanced around for a moment, then crossed over to her family graduation photograph. She picked it up and held it close. "I'd like to bring this too."

"Of course." He could hardly begrudge her the memento. "There's room in this bag."

She reached up and tucked the framed photo inside. Her fingers brushed his arm, and he could have sworn an electrical current zapped him. "They died two years ago," she said softly. "My mother died first, as you know, with complications from her poorly controlled diabetes. My father died three months later."

"I'm sorry to hear that." He wanted to reach out to her, but his hands were full.

She nodded and preceded him out of the house. As they headed back down the driveway, she stopped near her bright-blue SUV. "Can I park this in the garage?"

"Yes, that's fine." Jina had already cleared the garage, so he waited for her to pull the blue SUV inside. Then she stepped out and used a push-button code to close the garage door.

He placed her personal items in the back of his squad. The danger was over, but there was still a lot of activity in the area. Mostly his teammates looking for evidence of who had left the bomb behind. The house had been locked when they'd gotten there, so whoever had gained access had managed to make a duplicate house key.

Her former boyfriend Andrew Thomas? Maybe. He had already given the name to Joe and Rhy, but he would try to dig into the guy's background too.

"Where are we going?" she asked.

"I'm going to drop this squad at the police station first, then we'll pick up my SUV. From there, we'll head to the American Lodge. We use the place on a regular basis and know the owner. Gary has set aside a pair of connecting rooms."

She nodded. "Okay. But I hope they have internet access. I'll need to work while we're there."

That wasn't a surprise. "There's internet access. And Gary also has security cameras in place. You'll be safe there."

Her brow furrowed, and she gazed blankly out the window for a moment. "I don't understand why this is happening. I haven't hurt anyone, and my research is geared to helping people live long and healthy lives."

"I understand how anxious you are to get to work, but you need to think about every person you've come into contact with over the past few months. Anyone who has seemed envious of your research or upset with you in some way." He reached over to take her hand. "I'm convinced this guy knows you, Eve. He's someone you interacted with and relatively recently. The sooner you give me a list of names to investigate, the better."

"But I don't know anyone who would do this!" Her voice was strained. "I can't imagine anyone hates me enough to kill me!"

"He may hate your research more," he felt compelled to point out. "Killing you might be an added bonus."

"That's sick. Really sick." Her voice had dropped to a whisper.

"Yes, it is. And I'm sorry about that. But you're viewing this as a personal attack, and that is entirely possible. But targeting your work office and your home office tells me it's about the research itself."

"Diabetes research?" She shook her head in exasperation. "That's so inconceivable. Especially when you consider that this same person set two bombs. Not just setting fire to the office itself, but a *bomb*."

"I know it sounds over the top." He thought for a moment about the experiments they'd done in their chemistry lab. They hadn't made explosives, but they were talking about scientists who knew all about how to make things go boom. "Let's try this from another angle, then. What about professional jealousy? Is there some sort of hierarchy in place at the research institute? Anyone whose toes you stepped on recently?"

"Yes, the world of academia has a worse hierarchy system than most. Promotions are granted based on research papers and expertise in the lab. I was recently promoted to a full professor."

His pulse kicked up at that. "What were you before, a junior professor?"

She cracked a wan smile. "We call it associate professor. And there's also an adjunct professor, but that's more for those medical doctors who are also doing research."

"Are you telling me that you were promoted over a bunch of older guys?" he asked, trying to clarify the situation.

"Yes, exactly. I was one of six associate professors in my

field of study until I was promoted. Now there are five associate professors, and each of them has been working on their research for several years longer than I was." She shrugged. "I guess they might have a reason to be jealous."

"See? This is exactly what I'm talking about. You just mentioned five possible suspects." He felt certain they were onto something. Jealousy was the sort of emotion that could eat at a person over time until it became an obsession. "I need their names along with any others who have reason to be jealous or upset with you."

"Okay, I'll write down their names for you." She shot him an exasperated look. "But I can't imagine any of them setting a bomb in my office and in my home. That's a big step beyond rational."

"That's because you don't live in a world of violence like I do." He pulled into the parking lot of the precinct and turned to face her. "People can look and act normal up until the time that something pushes them over the edge." He reached for her hand again and felt the same zing of attraction. *Wrong time, wrong place, wrong woman,* he thought with a flash of annoyance. He didn't need this right now. With an effort, he thrust the weird awareness between them aside to focus on the present. "Please, Eve. I need you to trust me on this."

She searched his gaze for a long moment before nodding. "Okay, you have a point about the fact that I've lived a sheltered life. Yet it doesn't make sense that any of my colleagues would blow up the lab, impacting their own research too."

That much was true. "Still, jealousy and anger can be a powerful motivator."

"Okay." She glanced up, her gray eyes intense. "And

you should know that I do trust you, Grayson. More than anyone else."

"Good." He shouldn't have been so thrilled at her steadfast belief in him and his abilities.

Or so scared.

He realized he was in the same situation several of his teammates had been in over the past few months. Protecting an innocent woman from a crazy bomb-setting killer was an overwhelming responsibility.

And he could only pray he didn't fail in his job of keeping Eve safe.

CHAPTER THREE

Despite what Grayson believed, the idea that one of her colleagues could do something like this was incomprehensible. Yet she also understood that the sooner he checked into each of the associate professors she worked with, the sooner he would move on.

As promised Grayson stopped at the precinct. She followed him inside, looking around with blatant curiosity. She had never been in a police station before. It looked like something portrayed on police shows, yet she knew the officers and detectives were real, not actors.

How could this be happening? She sank into the closest chair, her knees once again threatening to buckle. She was a weakling. Her parents had doted on her, and she'd excelled in school, specifically in science. Studying hard and obtaining her doctorate degree at the age of twenty-three had not prepared her for this.

Grimly, she was forced to admit that nothing could have prepared her for this.

She stared down at her hands, willing them to stop

trembling. The danger was over, Grayson would keep her safe.

So why was she still shaking?

Eve had no idea how long she sat there, but she was startled badly when Grayson returned. He had changed into street clothes but still had the gun tucked in a holster looped on his belt. He also had a computer bag slung over one shoulder.

He looked good. Better than good. Drop-dead gorgeous. Which only made her more aware of her own bedraggled condition.

"Are you okay?" He looked at her with concern.

"Fine." She knew he could see through the lie but decided to put on a brave front anyway. "Although I'd still like to know if any of my colleagues were hurt or . . ." She couldn't finish.

"The initial report Rhy has so far is that there were no fatalities," Grayson said. "They are still searching of course. Do your colleagues get to work early?"

"Not always." She shook her head. "Some are night owls, coming in late, but then staying late."

He nodded. "I'm sorry I can't give you anything else yet. Are you ready to go?"

"Yes." When she rose to her feet, he took her hand. For some irrational reason, the warmth of his touch infused her with strength. She no longer felt as if she might keel over like a useless damsel in distress.

She followed Grayson through the building toward a door marked as an exit. Outside, the sun beat down on their heads as he led her to a black SUV. He surprised her by opening the passenger door for her.

"Thank you." She slid into the stifling hot car. Grayson left her door open to jog around to open the driver's side door, taking a moment to tuck his computer case in the back seat. Then he crossed over to the squad to retrieve the large bag holding her computer and notes along with her small suitcase, before sliding in beside her.

"It will take a minute for the vehicle to cool down." He shrugged as he waited for the air-conditioning to get up to speed. "No underground parking here at the cop shop."

"None for me either." She managed a smile. "Only the medical doctors working at the hospital rate high enough to have underground parking."

"Poor lowly researchers, huh?" he teased.

"Exactly." She turned one of the vents so that the cool air fanned her face.

After a minute, Grayson closed his driver's side door and put the car in gear. She closed her door, secured her seat belt, and rested back against the cushion. It seemed like days had passed since the early morning explosion rather than mere hours.

"Are you hungry?" Grayson glanced at her as they headed away from the relative safety of the police station. "There isn't any room service at the American Lodge, so we should pick up something for lunch along the way."

She wasn't hungry, but she understood that once they were tucked away in the motel, Grayson wouldn't want to leave. She forced herself to nod. "Sure. Whatever you'd like is okay with me."

He glanced at her. "Sub sandwiches? I seem to remember you're partial to a turkey club."

"Sounds good." She kept her tone light but was inwardly reeling from the fact that Grayson had remembered the one day they'd bumped into each other in the local sub sandwich shop. He was with one of his many cheerleader girlfriends—she'd lost track of which one—and had expected him to pretend not to know her. After all, she was hardly a member of the popular crowd.

Instead, he'd greeted her warmly, introducing her to his date as his amazing chemistry lab partner. She had flushed red with embarrassment and had barely been able to respond in a coherent way.

The memory of that brief meeting had stayed with her for a long time afterward, but she'd never imagined he'd remember it too.

"This should work." He pulled up into the drive-through window of the same submarine sandwich chain. He ordered four subs, two for each of them. Lunch and dinner, she assumed, but wasn't about to complain.

A few minutes later, he passed her the bag of food along with four bottles of water. "They have a mini fridge in the rooms, so cold sandwiches work best."

"You sound like you've spent quite a bit of time there."

He grinned. "Not the way you're thinking," he chided. "Our team uses the place as a safe house, nothing more."

She felt herself flush with embarrassment. "I didn't mean to imply . . ." She trailed off, unable to think of a way to salvage this train of thought.

"Sure, you did." He was still grinning. "I know I had a bit of a reputation in high school, but those days are long gone." The smile left his features, making him look sad. "I'm not involved with anyone, Eve."

"Okay." What could she say to that? She might want to know more about whether he'd been engaged, married, or divorced but managed to keep her mouth shut. He had a right to his privacy.

They arrived at the American Lodge ten minutes later. The white two-story building appeared nice enough. There were several cars in the parking lot, and she could see a family of four getting into a sedan with swimsuits and towels. They were likely heading to Bradford Beach to swim on the shore of Lake Michigan.

Something she'd never done despite living her entire life here in Milwaukee.

A few minutes later, she and Grayson had keys to rooms eleven and twelve on the second floor, near the staircase on the opposite end of the building from the lobby. They made two trips to the car and back for their respective computers, her oversized bag, suitcase, sandwiches, and water bottles. Seeing the suitcase, she quickly rummaged through the items she'd packed, choosing the comfy capri jeans and blue short-sleeved top. She ducked into the bathroom to change out of her business attire she'd been wearing beneath her lab coat. Shedding the clothing made her feel more feminine, and she wasn't entirely sure if that was a good thing or bad.

She was being ridiculous. Grayson would never be interested in a woman like her. And the sooner she made peace with that fact, the better.

Per Grayson's request, she unlocked her side of the connecting door. Then went to work on her computer. After a few minutes, he poked his head in, appearing surprised at how she'd already set up her computer on the small table.

"Ready to go to work, huh?" He held her gaze for a moment. "You look nice. We should eat first."

He'd noticed she'd changed? The minute the thought entered her mind she shrugged it off. What kind of cop would he be if he didn't pick up on details like clothing? He might not be an ace in chemistry, but he was still smart and street savvy. In truth, he was smart in ways she was likely very dumb. Like when it came to bombs. And crime in general.

"Okay." She would rather get to work on trying to figure out how much of her research had been lost in the explosion but knew he'd insist. Fuel was important for her brain, so she crossed the threshold to enter his room.

He had a laptop computer as well, but it was still lying on the bed. He'd set two of the sandwiches on the table, along with two water bottles. He gestured to one of the two chairs. "Please, have a seat."

She sat, trying to tuck her knees out of the way as he did the same. Their closeness was disconcerting, although she did her best to ignore it. She bowed her head and clasped her hands in her lap, silently giving thanks to the Lord Jesus for providing this food and for keeping them safe.

When she looked up, Grayson had his hands folded in his lap, too, waiting. She flushed again, seemingly off balance when it came to him. "I, uh, was taught to pray before meals."

He nodded. "Several of my teammates do too."

But he didn't? She decided not to ask, taking a moment to unwrap her sandwich. They ate in silence for a few minutes.

"How long do you think we'll need to stay here?" she asked.

"As long as it takes," he answered with a shrug.

She frowned. "As long as it takes to what? Find the person responsible for setting those bombs?"

"Yep." He took a bite of his sandwich. "I hope to start narrowing the suspect pool as soon as we're finished eating."

She wouldn't be the only one working then; Grayson would do his part too. And that meant he needed the names of her colleagues.

Rising to her feet, she crossed back into her room for a pencil and pad of sticky notes. Between bites, she listed the five names of the assistant professors that could be harboring some resentment regarding her promotion.

She handed the note to Grayson, he looked down at the names with interest. "Anyone else you can think of who might be jealous of your work?"

She sighed, chewing slowly. Then shrugged and reached for the pencil again, jotting down the name of Dave Firestein. "This professor does the same sort of research I do. He's located in Madison, working out of their lab. We share ideas on occasion, but I'm using a different approach compared to his." She hesitated, then added, "He was the one who arranged for this live presentation. I was honored to speak to my fellow colleagues about a subject I'm so passionate about."

Grayson took that sticky note too. "Have you met this Dave Firestein in person? Or do you mostly talk on the phone and through video conferences?"

"I've met him in person several times," she admitted. "But that's mostly at research conferences."

"Hmm." Grayson put the two sticky notes together. "Anyone else?"

She grimaced. "I told you about the extremist groups. There was an animal rights group that camped outside the research institute a couple of weeks ago. I don't know anything about them, though. Other than what I read on their signs."

"Which group was it?" Grayson asked.

She scribbled the abbreviation on a third sticky note and handed it over. "I don't know how you could possibly track down which members were picketing outside the research institute a few weeks ago."

"You'd be surprised, most of these animal rights organizations are proud of the work they do, and they don't mind sharing their names and things they've done."

She finished her sandwich and took another sip of water. "I hope it's not them because I love animals, especially dogs. I would never harm them. How could anyone who claims to love animals go to the lengths of planting a bomb in my office and in my home?"

"Extremist groups can attract unstable people," he said with a shrug. "Most of them are true believers of their cause and wouldn't harm anyone. But there could be someone with a screw loose who joined the group. Besides, we don't know for sure they're involved in this; it's one avenue to pursue."

"Yes, I know." She sat back, toying with her water bottle. No matter how hard she tried, she couldn't come up with anyone else who could possibly hate her enough to set two bombs intended to kill her. And to put the rest of her colleagues in jeopardy.

The whole situation made her head hurt.

Finally, she capped her water bottle and rose to her feet. "I have work to do."

Grayson stood, too, moving out of the way so she could edge past him. It took all of her willpower not to throw herself into his arms, seeking reassurance that everything would turn out okay.

Normally, getting lost in her work was a surefire way to push the outside world aside. But not today.

Not with Grayson moving around in the next room.

She closed her eyes. She absolutely needed to get over this ridiculous crush she had on the guy. And soon.

Before she made a giant fool out of herself.

DIGGING into Eve's work colleagues wasn't as difficult as Grayson had anticipated. These guys were proud of their research studies and wanted everyone to know it. He found all the researchers listed on the main page of the research institute, along with a photograph. The pictures were enough to help him estimate their age as he painstakingly performed criminal background checks on each one.

One guy, Geoff Abbott, had a ticket for driving while intoxicated when he was nineteen years old. Probably not an indication of criminal intent, but he still made a note about it. The next three guys were clean, but the last one, a Nick Strong, had a surprising arrest for assault and battery, also when he was nineteen.

He would ask the team's tech specialist, Gabe Melrose, to get him more information on both cases, although he mentally placed Nick Strong at the top of the list. If the guy had lost his temper once, he could easily do it again.

Granted, placing bombs was a task generally well planned ahead of time, not done in a spur-of-the-moment flash of anger. But for all he knew. Nick Strong had learned to rein in his temper.

When he'd finished a surface look at her colleagues, hoping they'd survived the blast, he did the same background check on associate professor Dave Firestein. The Madison professor was also clean.

He'd need to dig deeper into their social media sites, but he decided to go to the animal rights group first. He found the website without difficulty and clicked on their news and events page.

The group did some great work, rescuing dogs and cats from horrible owners, breaking up dog-fighting rings. But it didn't take long for him to find the picture of the dozen people who had camped outside the research institute two weeks ago.

He blew up the photograph, examining each member's face closely before reaching for his phone. The photograph was clear enough for facial recognition, so he called the team's tech guru Gabe Melrose.

"What's going on, Grayson?" Gabe asked.

"I need your help running twelve faces through the facial rec program."

Gabe sighed. "Okay, shoot me their pictures."

"They happen to all be in one large photograph. Do you have a minute? I'll show you where to find it."

"Go ahead," Gabe said. "I'm ready."

He quickly gave Gabe the website and walked him through to the picture of interest. "See the group photo? This was taken outside the research institute two weeks ago."

"Hmm. I see it. This will take a little time," Gabe said. "I can do it, but I'll have to manipulate the pictures a bit first to sharpen them up. I hope you don't expect the names in an hour."

"I'd like them as soon as possible, but I understand it may take some time." He tried to soothe Gabe's ruffled feathers. "Oh, and there's another thing. I need the full arrest reports on a Geoff Abbott and Nick Strong. Abbott was charged with DUI and Strong for assault and battery."

"Hang on a minute." Grayson could hear Gabe clicking on the keyboard. "I found them."

"Great. Shoot them my way and then call me when you have the list of names to match the photographs of the animal rights group, okay?"

"Yeah, yeah." Gabe sounded irked. "It's not like I'm sitting around eating donuts over here."

"I would never say that," he protested. "You're a rock star, Gabe. Thanks." Grayson disconnected from the call before Gabe could say anything more. The guy was a whizz at tech stuff, and despite his protests, Grayson knew Gabe would dig into the task immediately if nothing more than to prove himself worthy. The guy took their requests as personal challenges.

He went back to dig into each suspect's social media sites. That took a lot of toggling back and forth to compare photographs, but he located the social media pages he was looking for.

Except for one. Nick Strong.

Well, well, wasn't that interesting? The professor with a temper avoided social media. Granted, he and his teammates didn't have social media pages either. Most cops tended to avoid them. But he had created a page without a photograph just so he could search the site.

He checked his email, but there were no arrest reports from Gabe yet. He rose and stretched, realizing several hours had passed. Crossing to the connecting door, he looked at Eve. He smiled when he saw at least ten sticky notes strewn about her workspace.

It seemed as if the pretty professor had to write notes to herself in order to work. And why he found that adorable, he had no idea.

"Eve?"

She startled so badly she slammed her knee against the leg of the table. "What?" She sounded cross as she rubbed at her injured knee. "Is that a cop thing, to sneak up on people?"

"I wasn't trying to scare you, but I wanted your input on a guy named Nick Strong." He edged closer into the room. "Do you need ice for your knee?"

"No." She frowned and stopped massaging the injury. "What about Nick?"

"He was charged with assault and battery," he said.

Her eyes rounded in shock. "No way! When?"

"He was nineteen, so almost fifteen years ago," he quickly clarified. "I don't have the full arrest report yet, so I'm not sure what happened."

"Fifteen years ago?" She looked at him as if he were crazy. "What does an arrest record from fifteen years ago have to do with this? You think punching some guy in a bar is a stepping stone to planting bombs?"

"Is that what happened? He told you he punched someone in a bar?"

"No, he didn't tell me anything. I have no idea what happened." She waved a hand impatiently. "But that's the sort of thing a nineteen-year-old might do."

"Nineteen isn't old enough to be in a bar," he pointed out.

She sighed loudly. "Look, Grayson, I understand you're trying to investigate this thing, and I appreciate that. But I'm telling you, the men I work with are dedicated scientists. I can't see how some crime from fifteen years ago has any bearing on what is happening now."

"I thought you trusted me?" He was getting tired of hearing her defend her coworkers. "This happens to be my area of expertise, remember?"

A hint of movement outside the motel room window caught his eye. He frowned and moved closer, peering through the opening in the curtains. He scanned the parking lot but didn't see anything suspicious.

He reached for his phone and called Gary Campbell. "Are your security cameras on?" he asked.

"Yes, why?" Gary sounded concerned. "Did you see something?"

"Check the cameras across from our rooms," he directed. Then to Eve, he said, "Gather your notes and shut down your computer. We may have to leave in a hurry."

To her credit, Eve didn't argue. She picked up all her sticky notes and shoved them into the computer bag along with the laptop itself.

"First camera is clear." He could hear Gary using a computer in the background, no doubt pulling up one video camera at a time. Then Gary whistled. "Grayson? You have trouble. An armed man ducked behind the trees across from your room."

"Call Rhy, tell him we need backup ASAP." He disconnected from the call, grabbed Eve's computer case, and then took her arm. "Go to the bathroom and climb into the tub. Take your large bag holding the computer with you and use it as a shield, if necessary, understand?"

"The tub?" She looked surprised by the directive, but when he gave her a little push toward the bathroom, she quickly complied, holding the computer to her chest. Seconds later, she disappeared into the bathroom.

"Grayson? Rhy wants you to know Cassidy and Flynn are on the way," Gary said. "ETA is roughly seven minutes."

"Thanks. Stay in the lobby behind the counter and away from the doors." He peered through the curtains again. He knew the trees made for a good hiding spot; they'd been used in the past by other bad guys. And now that it was summertime, the leaves offered plenty of coverage, making it that much more difficult to see who might be hiding up there.

As he watched and waited, his mind whirled. How had their location been found? He knew they weren't followed.

Eve's computer? Maybe. It was the only possibility that made sense.

He pulled his sidearm and moved to the side of the window farthest from the door. Depending on the weapon, the perp could easily shoot through the wall, taking him out of commission. That had been done in the past by a perp attempting to shoot Joe and Elly too.

He didn't like this. Not one bit.

"Grayson? Where are you?" Eve called. "I thought you were coming in here too?"

"Soon," he lied with a wince. "Stay down in the bathtub. Our backup is on the way." Seven minutes could easily be six minutes too late.

He drew in his breath and let it out slowly, then moved the curtain just enough to see outside. Keeping his gaze on the trees directly across from their room, he searched for a sign of movement. There was a slight breeze that shuffled the leaves on occasion, so he tried to look for signs of unnatural movement.

There! What appeared to be an elbow poking out from the tree trunk about six feet off the ground flashed in his line of sight. He pressed the nose of his sidearm against the window, but then the target was gone.

Grayson stayed right where he was, hoping the perp would have to show himself again to take another shot at them.

There was another slight movement, this time higher up in the tree. He blinked, realizing the shooter had somehow managed to get up into the tree without his noticing. Maybe he'd seen a knee, not an elbow.

He waited with infinite patience for another glimpse of the perp. Another knee came into view. Then there was the crack of gunfire.

He didn't hesitate to return fire, the rounds piercing the glass window.

The man in the tree dropped to the ground and then began to run. Grayson ran to the door and wrenched it open, intending to follow, but then caught himself.

What if there were two perps? One intended to draw him out, the other waiting for the opportunity to get to Eve?

He slammed the door and locked it, then returned to the window to watch.

Staying put and allowing his teammates to give chase was the hardest thing he'd ever had to do.

CHAPTER FOUR

Being in the bathtub with her bulky bag protecting her head was extremely uncomfortable. Listening intently, Eve thought she heard Grayson talking. Then there was the sharp report of gunfire.

Gunfire that was once again intended for her.

She silently prayed for God's shield of strength and for Grayson and the other officers who were likely on the way to be safe from harm.

First bombs, now guns.

Why? Even an animal rights activist wouldn't go this far, would they?

For long seconds, there was nothing but silence. The muscles in her arms trembled with exertion from holding up her shoulder bag filled with her work notes and computer.

Just when she thought she couldn't stand it there for another minute, she heard a knock at the door. "Eve? You can come out now."

"Thank You, Lord Jesus," she silently whispered, lowering the bag to the bottom of the tub and shaking out her arms.

"Eve?" Grayson's tone sounded urgent. "Are you okay? I'm coming in."

"I'm fine." She wasn't but understood he was talking about her physical condition, not her emotional state. She levered herself upright as Grayson opened the door and peered inside.

He rushed over to give her a hand. She did her best to appear calm but knew her hands were shaking.

She wasn't cut out for this sort of thing. Watching explosions, searching for bombs, running from danger. This wasn't normal for her.

For anyone, really. Except Grayson and his fellow teammates.

"Hey, you look pale." Grayson's dark eyes searched hers. "You're safe, Eve. The gunman is gone."

"They didn't catch him?" she asked, trying not to feel deflated.

"Not yet." His gaze was sympathetic. "Trust me, we want him as badly as you do."

"I know." She swallowed her disappointment. None of this was his fault. In fact, Grayson had saved her life.

Again.

"Stay close." He reached for her oversized bag and slung it over his shoulder as if it were filled with cotton balls. "Cassidy and Flynn are going to help us get out of here."

Sticking close wouldn't be a problem. If anything, she wished she could absorb even a fraction of his strength and determination.

Grayson took her bag and led the way through the motel room, toward the door. He urged her to stay up against the wall as he opened the door and looked outside. After a few seconds, he stepped through the opening. "It's clear."

She followed him down the stairs to the main level where a squad was waiting near Grayson's black SUV. Two officers, male and female, stood there in full gear. They were scanning the area intently as she and Grayson joined them.

"Your SUV may be compromised," Cassidy said. "Rhy wants us to take you to the precinct to get another vehicle."

"I'm fairly certain the perp tracked us here by Eve's computer access, but I agree we should swap vehicles just to be safe," Grayson said.

"My computer?" She stared at him. "You really think so?"

"Yeah, it's the only thing that makes sense." Grayson shrugged. "I know we weren't followed, and it took some time for the bad guys to find us."

Tracking her computer via the internet was not something she'd anticipated. And the thought filled her with dread. "That means I can't work on my research while we're hiding out."

"I'm afraid not." Grayson rested his hand in the hollow of her back. "I'm sorry, Eve. But we need to keep you safe and secure, which entails staying off-grid."

Off-grid. It was depressing how isolating that sounded. Yet how could she argue? Especially after this most recent incident?

"Everyone okay?" Gary asked as he emerged from the lobby.

"Yes, but your window is broken. Again," Grayson said apologetically.

"You promised not to bring danger," Gary groused. He glanced up at the window and sighed. "I'll need to get that repaired before the weekend."

"I'll take care of the cost," Grayson offered.

"Yeah, yeah." Gary waved a hand. "I know you guys are good about that. I just don't want to lose the weekend business."

Eve felt terrible at the thought of Gary losing his business. "I can help pay too. I feel responsible."

"It's not your fault," Grayson assured her. "I should have anticipated the computer connection being tracked."

"Grayson?" Flynn gestured to the squad. "Time to get Dr. Shaw out of here."

"Coming." He urged her toward the squad, then paused and tossed a key fob to Cassidy. "Be careful driving it back."

"I'll be fine." Cassidy grinned. "I'll take a detour and try to pick up a tail. Maybe we'll get this guy yet."

"We can only hope," Grayson muttered as he stored her bag in the back seat. "Meet you at the precinct."

Eve knew they were mostly joking, but it was just more proof of how they didn't hesitate to put their lives on the line to protect the public.

To protect her.

Being unable to work on her research was depressing, but she didn't want to cause anyone harm either.

She stared blindly out the window as Flynn navigated the streets of Brookland to head back to the precinct. She was lost in thought, but then a familiar home caught her eye. "That's where my boss lives."

"Your boss?" Grayson swiveled in the front passenger seat to look at her curiously. "You haven't mentioned him."

"Why would I?" She frowned. "He gets some credit for having me on his team."

"And you don't think he might be jealous of your work?" Grayson asked.

"He pays me to do my work, why would he be envious of it?" She pressed her fingertips into her temple in a vain effort to ward off another nagging headache. "Fine, you want to investigate him too? His name is Dr. Roger C. Cannon. Maybe he has unpaid parking tickets from fifteen years ago."

She caught the surprise in Flynn's gaze as he glanced at her in the rearview mirror. She forced herself to swallow her anger. Maybe it was a cop's job to look at all the people around her as potential suspects, no matter how absurd it might be.

But she didn't have to like it.

"Unpaid parking tickets don't show up in the criminal database," Grayson responded evenly. "And I know you're having trouble with seeing your colleagues in a bad light, but we still need to check them out. Including your boss. And anyone else you can think of who might be involved in this."

"That's just it," she said wearily. "I don't think any of them are involved in this. Why would they be? As I said before, they use the same research lab I do. A lab full of very expensive equipment. And we don't even know if any of them were injured in the blast, remember?"

"I know. I'm hoping to get some additional information on that soon. And you should know that people are not always logical," Grayson said. "Emotions can run amok and cause people to act out impulsively."

"Fine. Have it your way." She hated knowing he was right. She didn't say anything more, still grappling with how she'd gotten to this point. Her life was boring. Routine. Uneventful.

Earlier today her biggest concern was being rear-ended by a harried mother of three.

Now she'd been targeted by two bombs and gunfire.

The scenery outside her window passed in a blur. She

had no idea where they would go next. Or how long this would take.

She silently prayed that Grayson and the others would find and arrest the person responsible so she could return to her dull, boring, and routine life.

GRAYSON EXCHANGED KNOWING looks with Flynn. Eve was taking this recent attempt against her extremely hard, and honestly, he couldn't blame her.

She didn't deserve this. No one did. But he didn't care how much she admired the people she worked with, he firmly believed one of them was responsible.

These attacks were personal. Targeting both her and her research. He wondered what would happen to her field of study if she was unable to keep working on it.

Would it fizzle out? Or would someone else step in to pick up where she had left off?

Maybe that was another angle to consider. At this point, he'd take any and all theories under advisement. Because the sad truth was that other than jealousy as a motivation, they were running out of leads.

Oh, he'd check out her boss, but the brief work he'd done on her colleagues hadn't yielded anything useful. Two possible suspects, but even that was a stretch.

Flynn pulled up to the side entrance of the building. "You want to go inside? Or wait here for me to grab a key? I think the Jeep is available now that it's been fixed."

"We'll go inside for a few minutes. I need to brief Rhy and Joe on the American Lodge incident." He also wanted to check on Gabe Melrose's progress on the facial recognition of the animal rights group.

Flynn shrugged and killed the engine. "Okay, let's go."

Grayson pushed out of the passenger seat and opened the back door for Eve. She slid out from the squad without meeting his gaze. Then turned to grab her bag. He wasn't sure why she was upset with him for doing his job, but he did his best to shrug it off.

He led the way inside, with Flynn following behind Eve. They took up protective positions by instinct and force of habit. Eve went over to sit at the same desk she had before.

"I won't be long," he said.

She nodded wordlessly. He hesitated, wondering if there was something more he should say, then decided to leave it alone.

Eve had lost her office, some of her research, access to her lab and to her home. She was entitled to be a little cranky.

"Grayson? What happened?" Rhy asked with concern.

He filled his boss in on the gunman who'd staked out the American Lodge. "I take full responsibility," he added. "It never occurred to me that they'd track Eve's computer."

"I understand; at least no one was hurt. Besides, it is a very different MO for this guy to come after her with a gun after planting two bombs," Rhy mused.

"Exactly." Grayson shook his head. "I was leaning toward one of the animal rights people going rogue, but now I think we need to remain focused on her colleagues. I'm sure she logged into the computer system within the Milwaukee College of Medical Research, and who would know that better than someone she works with?"

"Agreed." Rhy searched his gaze. "We got word that two assistant professors were in the elevator when the bomb went off. They were both rescued and are relatively unharmed. It's interesting that no one died from the blast. Almost as if it was an inside job."

No kidding. "Which professors?" he asked.

"Hang on." Rhy checked his notes. "Allan Ballard and Larry Kimmel."

He nodded, thinking that the fact that they were in the building when the bomb went off indicated they were probably not involved. "Thanks."

"You okay to stay with Dr. Shaw?" Rhy asked. "Or do you want to swap with one of the others?"

"I'll stay with Eve," he answered quickly. It didn't make sense, but he couldn't bring himself to leave her with anyone else. "Like you said, we have a rapport."

"Fine with me." Rhy glanced at his watch. "Sorry, I have a meeting with Michaels shortly. Take Eve to another hotel, and this time stay off the radar. Don't leave an electronic trail."

"Roger that. Thanks." Grayson left his boss, poking his head into Melrose's office. "Hey, did you find anything yet?"

"I told you I wouldn't have results in an hour," Gabe shot back. "I'm working on it, okay? Be satisfied with the arrest reports."

He'd been so busy he hadn't checked his email. Lifting his phone, he thumbed the screen until he found Gabe's email. "I see them. Thanks. Call me when you have something to share."

Melrose sighed loudly and went back to work. Over Gabe's shoulder he could see that he was fine-tuning one of the faces in the group photo. He wondered if this was the first photograph Gabe had started working on but wisely decided not to ask.

He returned to the main area where he found Flynn

perched on the corner of the desk chatting with Eve. Out of nowhere, a flash of jealousy hit hard.

It was an unfamiliar emotion. He'd always been on the receiving end of a woman's attention, not the other way around. The last time he'd been rebuffed by someone was nearly ten years ago, when Eve had seemed oblivious to his interest.

He shook off the unwelcome thought. They weren't in high school anymore. And he had no claim on Eve or anyone else. He needed to stay focused on the issue at hand, not on his wayward hormones.

"Did Rhy have any words of wisdom?" Flynn asked as he approached.

"Just that we should find another place to stay." He was relieved he sounded normal. "I was thinking about using the City Central Hotel downtown."

"Good choice." Flynn stood. "I grabbed the Jeep keys; it's running like a charm after being repaired from the damage it sustained last month. Do you want me to ride shotgun?"

"No need." The refusal came out a little too fast. "We'll be fine with a clean ride."

"Okay." Thankfully, Flynn didn't take offense. A few months ago, Flynn had almost resigned from the tactical team for unwittingly playing a role in placing Steele in danger. Rhy had assured Flynn he wasn't at fault, and it seemed as if Flynn finally agreed. "Here you go." Flynn held out the Jeep key fob. "It's parked at the end of the lot."

"I saw it." He glanced at Eve who didn't seem as upset as earlier. "Do you mind hitting the road?"

"I'm ready." She rose to her feet, then placed a hand on his arm. "I'm sorry. I shouldn't take my frustration out on you."

"I can take it." He grinned, feeling 100 percent lighter at her apology. "I'm here for you no matter what."

"I know." She surprised him by going up on her tiptoes to kiss his cheek. "Thanks for saving my life. Again."

"Ah, sure. Of course." He was flustered by her sweet caress. He glanced at Flynn who was watching their interaction with a slightly amused and knowing look. As if he'd said something to smooth things over with Eve.

And if so, he owed the guy a big fat thank-you.

"This way." He gestured to the door they'd used on the way in.

"I was just getting used to the air-conditioning." She lifted her bag and tucked a strand of hair behind her ear. "I guess you can tell I don't spend a lot of time outside."

He glanced at her. "You do important work, Eve. I have the opposite kind of job, one that cannot be done from a desk." And that was exactly why he loved being a cop. Most of the time. Their tactical team found themselves in dicey situations, which were never boring. He valued his life and those of his teammates, but at the same time, he'd never survive in one of those nine-to-five office jobs.

Not for any amount of money.

"By the way, no one was injured in the blast," he said. "Two of your colleagues, Allan Ballard and Larry Kimmel, were in the elevator at the time your office exploded. They were not hurt."

"I'm very thankful for that." She looked relieved by the news. He led the way outside to the Jeep, which was also black. "Don't you drive anything with color?" she asked as he opened the passenger door for him.

"No. Black blends in with the night. And there are a lot of black vehicles out there that provide anonymity."

Her eyes widened. "I guess I hadn't thought of that."

He nodded. "That's not the world you live in, Eve. But it is mine. Your bright-blue SUV made me cringe."

"I thought maybe you had something against blue," she said thoughtfully, setting her bag on the floor between her feet.

"Not at all." He left her door open to round the back of the vehicle. He started the engine, and once again, they waited a moment for the heat to disperse before closing the doors and hitting the road.

Grayson took several turns, went around the block, and headed north before turning to go east toward the lakefront. He knew they hadn't been followed to the American Lodge but decided to take extra precautions anyway.

"Is that Lake Michigan?" Eve craned her neck to see better. "It's so pretty."

He frowned. "You've never been to the lakefront?"

"I flew over it a few times heading to conferences, but I haven't actually been down there myself, no." She spoke absently, as if there were plenty of people in Milwaukee who had never gone to the lakefront.

"I'll take you down on a Saturday afternoon when this is over." He would love nothing more than to take her now, but that wasn't an option. Besides, he wanted to spend time with her when he didn't have to constantly be on the lookout for danger. "You'll love it."

"I—uh, okay." She flushed a little as she settled back in her seat. "You must think I'm lame."

"Never said that." He did think she was overly sheltered while growing up, and maybe a bit too focused on her work now that she was an adult. He understood being driven to succeed, but she had to relax sometime. "It wouldn't hurt to do something for fun occasionally. There are all kinds of things to do down there. Rent a paddleboat, ride bikes, play beach volleyball. Or simply hang out on the beach in the sun."

She nodded but didn't say anything more, giving him the distinct impression she'd never done any of those things. It occurred to him that once this nightmare was over, he would love to show Eve the parts of the city she'd never experienced. For now, he let the subject drop as he navigated the side streets toward the Milwaukee County Courthouse and the City Central Hotel.

The two-story hotel was not overly impressive, but its location near the courthouse made it useful for the DA's office to have witnesses stay there during long trials. And it was one of the usual places, like the American Lodge, that Rhy, Joe, and the rest of the team used to stay off-grid.

It didn't take long to obtain one of their first-floor suites. He put the room in his name and on his credit card. After lugging Eve's bag and his computer case inside, he closed and double locked the door.

"We forgot our sub sandwiches," Eve said with a frown. "I hate wasting food."

"That's okay; there's a small room service menu available. I'll call Gary and let him know he and his staff can eat the subs." He set her bag on the couch, then stepped over to the small table to set up his computer. Now that they were situated and safe, he was anxious to review the arrest reports Gabe had sent.

"Sure, you get to work on your computer, but I don't." Eve sighed, then waved a hand. "Sorry, ignore my whining. It's fine. I'll just review my notes."

He knew she wasn't mad at him but at the situation. "Maybe reviewing your notes will bring back some of the ideas you had jotted down on your sticky notes in your office."

"I hope so." She sat on the sofa and dug in her bag. "Although I think better when I have multiple screens open on my laptop at the same time."

She did? Hard to imagine, he could barely handle working on one screen at a time. Leaving her to it, he logged into his email and read through the DUI report from associate professor Geoff Abbott. The guy was driving with a leaky muffler, which was how he got pulled over, then blew a one point zero on the breathalyzer test. He was given a citation mostly because he was underage and driving.

He moved on to the next report on the assault and battery charges against Nick Strong. It wasn't a bar fight, but rather a domestic situation where he apparently slugged his former girlfriend's new boyfriend in the face.

Jealousy and anger, a dangerous mix. But enough to have the guy planting bombs in Eve's workplace and home office? Hard to say. But he would absolutely leave Nick Strong on the suspect list for now, especially since he seemed to be the jealous type.

He glanced over to where Eve was sitting on the sofa staring into space with at least five pads of sticky notes in her lap. After a long moment, she picked up her pencil and made a notation on a yellow sticky note, then set that one aside. Smiling to himself, he realized she didn't need a computer screen as long as she had all those brightly colored sticky notes.

Turning back to his computer, he searched for another email from Gabe Melrose but didn't find one. He was tempted to call the tech specialist to tell him to send the names as soon as he had them. Then he decided patience was a virtue and went back to the unsatisfactory task of searching social media sites.

It was painfully slow work, and by the time he got

through searching on Eve's boss, Roger C. Cannon, he wanted to claw his eyes out of his head.

Roger C. Cannon had a second wife who was young, pretty, and wore slinky gowns at various charity events. He had no idea what being the director of the research institute paid, but it was obviously far more than he made as a cop.

Finding nothing of interest there, he picked up his phone. As if Gabe had sensed his impatience, his name flashed on the screen. "Okay, I have five names for you so far. Are you ready?"

He searched for paper and a pencil, but of course, he didn't find one. He pulled up a blank document on the computer screen. "Yup, go ahead."

"Robert Kevin Anderson, he's the first guy on the left in the back row. Then we have Sean Joseph O'Malley, he's the next guy over. The third is a guy by the name of Terrance Anthony Motors. The fourth is Kenneth James Kratz. And the last guy is Michael Harold Jones."

He typed furiously as Gabe talked. "What about dates of birth on these guys? I'll need that to dig into their criminal backgrounds."

"Oh yeah, hang on. I'll send you those with the names in an email." Gabe's fingers tapped on the keyboard. "One thing you should know is that Sean Joseph O'Malley has dual citizenship with the USA and Ireland."

"You think he learned how to set bombs in Ireland?" he asked dubiously.

"What? No, just that he likely has friends across the pond that he could go to if he got in trouble." Gabe chuckled. "He's far too young to be part of the Ireland Republic Army."

"I see. Okay, thanks. This is great work, Gabe. I'm grateful to have these names to work on."

"I'll keep going on the others," Gabe said. "Rhy approved some overtime for me on this."

Rhy was good that way and would likely smooth the extra time over with their assistant chief, Michaels. One good thing about their tactical team was that they had exceptional results, closing some big cases. "Great, thanks again." He ended the call and quickly looked at his email again.

"What did you find out?" Eve hovered near his right shoulder.

Glancing up at her, he found her peering at his screen. "I have five names from that animal rights group photo."

She pulled up a chair to sit beside him. "Can I watch?"

He wanted to tell her to go back to the sofa but nodded. She had an orange sticky note stuck to her shirt. She blushed when he peeled it off and set it aside. "Sure, if you like." He decided to start inputting the names in order. No surprise to find both criminal backgrounds on Robert K. Anderson and Sean J. O'Malley were clean. He put in the third name, and then the fourth. Still nothing.

To his surprise the fifth name, Michael Harold Jones, popped up with several criminal violations. Leaning forward, he clicked on the case file of the most recent citation.

Breaking and entering along with destruction of private property. Charges that were filed about a year ago. He turned to look at Eve. "I think we may have found another possible suspect."

"Setting off a bomb is a far crime from breaking and entering and property damage," she protested.

"These are the crimes they were able to prove," he said slowly. "He could have done other things too." He checked the guy's address and found he lived in Milwaukee.

He reached for his phone to call Joe. The guy's criminal past may not be enough for a search warrant, but at the very least, they could bring Michael Harold Jones in for a police interview.

They needed something to go on very soon. And this guy was their most likely candidate.

CHAPTER FIVE

Eve stared at the photo of Michael Harold Jones, trying to imagine the ordinary-looking man placing a bomb in her office and in her home. There was something vaguely familiar about him, but she couldn't place it. Maybe he had been one of the sign-holding demonstrators she'd walked past on her way into the office a couple of weeks ago.

Or maybe her imagination was working overtime, and she'd never seen this man before in her life. Either way, she was having trouble understanding why he wanted to kill her.

If he was even the one behind these attacks. It didn't seem logical; then again, setting bombs wasn't rational no matter how you looked at it.

She rose and moved away from the computer, wrapping her arms around her waist. In some ways, she hoped Michael Harold Jones was responsible. If so, she was one step closer to returning to her normal, boring life.

And her research.

It was troubling to realize she didn't know what to do with herself without the ability to lose herself in her research. As if her life had no meaning aside from her diabetes work. Which she knew was not true. She attended church. She knew God was watching out for her and for the rest of the tactical team.

So why was she feeling as if she were adrift at sea? In a boat without a life jacket while not knowing how to swim? She didn't like feeling useless.

"Rhy?" Grayson's voice interrupted her thoughts. "We need to bring in a guy by the name of Michael Harold Jones. He lives in Milwaukee and is a possible suspect in setting the bombs."

She paced the length of the room, listening as Grayson discussed arrangements to interview the animal rights suspect.

"Yes, that should work. I should have realized Mitch Callahan would need to interview Eve."

Who was Mitch Callahan? She didn't remember hearing the name before. It was annoying to be discussed as if she wasn't standing right there, but she reminded herself that she was a victim. Of course, Grayson would be taking a lead on things.

"Okay, we can be there in fifteen. Thanks." He ended the call and stood to face her. "We need to head back to the precinct."

"I heard. Who is Mitch Callahan?"

"He's the arson investigator who will help pinpoint the location and type of device that was set." Grayson's gaze was serious. "It's my fault I didn't think to contact him sooner. I should have known he'd be called to the scene."

"You can't think of everything." She grabbed her errant sticky note, then looped her oversize bag onto her shoulder. "I'm ready."

"You can leave that here if you like." Grayson gestured to the bag.

"I'd rather keep it with me." Her notes and laptop were priceless now that her office had been blown into smithereens. "Please," she added when it looked as if he might argue.

"I'll carry it for you." He held out his hand.

"I have it." She clung to the bag handle as if it were a lifeline. "Let's just get this over with."

He nodded and held the door open for her. They didn't speak as they headed outside to the black Jeep.

This would be her third trip to the police station in one day. After setting the bag on the floor between her feet, she clipped her seat belt.

The June sun was still high in the sky, as they were close to the summer solstice. Her stomach rumbled with hunger, but she ignored it. It seemed absurd to want dinner at a time like this.

As promised, they arrived at the precinct within fifteen minutes. She knew her way around now and was about to go to her usual desk when Grayson guided her toward an interview room. "Mitch is waiting."

"Okay." Flustered, she opened the door to see a tall blond-haired man standing at one side of the table.

"Dr. Shaw, it's a pleasure to meet you." Mitch extended his hand, so she took it. "I'm sorry it has to be under these circumstances."

"Thanks." She sat in the empty chair, setting her bag at her feet. "You're absolutely sure there are no casualties from the blast?"

"A few people in the offices below yours suffered minor injuries, but it appears the early morning hour was a blessing as there were not many people around." Mitch held her gaze. "Is that usual for the research institute? To have the building mostly empty at seven in the morning?"

She nodded. "Yes. I was going in early for my online presentation, but normally, I get to work around eight. So do many of the others. We don't punch a clock, if that's what you're asking."

"I suspect that the timing of the blast was to target you specifically since there were no other victims," Mitch said. "And from what I can tell, your desk was tucked in the corner where you could sit and look out the window."

"That's true too." She shivered despite the warmth. "I guess it's a good thing this bomber only wanted to hurt me."

"It's not good that anyone wants to hurt you, but yes, it seems as if this perp tried to minimize the impact." Mitch leaned forward. "I know Grayson and the others have already asked, but I need to hear it from you. Do you have any idea who set these bombs?"

"I don't. I wish I could point you in the right direction." She glanced at Grayson who gave her an encouraging nod. "I gave Grayson—er, Officer Clark the names of my colleagues, my competitors so to speak, and mentioned the animal rights group that camped outside the building a few weeks ago. He's been looking into them."

"I know, I got an update from Rhy on that." Mitch nodded at Grayson. "I'll poke around in their backgrounds too. And I understand Michael Harold Jones is being picked up for an interview."

"He's one of the animal rights activists and has a previous charge of breaking and entering along with destruction of private property." Grayson shrugged. "I figure it's a place to start."

"I agree," Mitch said. She was surprised that the arson

investigator thought along the same lines as Grayson. "He could have done other things we're not aware of."

It must be exhausting to expect the worst of people. But she didn't say anything more. "Barbara the receptionist wasn't hurt?" she asked.

Mitch glanced at his notes. "It appears Barbara Copland had the day off. So yes, she's fine."

She frowned, realizing Barbara hadn't mentioned having the day off. Although really, it wasn't her job to keep track of the receptionist's schedule. "Good. I'm glad to hear it."

Mitch went through a few more questions similar to the ones Grayson had asked. She dutifully answered them all. When she was finished, Grayson and Mitch exchanged a long glance.

"Anything I missed?" Mitch asked.

Grayson shook his head. "No. I'm happy to share all the information I've gathered thus far."

"I'll keep you in the loop too," Mitch said. "Better for us to work this thing together. Good catch on finding the device in her home office." Mitch turned to face her. "Any other place you go on a regular basis? The gym? A coffee shop?"

"No." She flushed with embarrassment. "I pretty much work, eat, and sleep."

Mitch nodded without commenting on her lack of social life. "Unfortunately, I won't be able to dig into the scene further until tomorrow or Thursday. By then it should have cooled off enough for me to sift through the debris."

"Understood." Grayson pulled out his phone. "Looks like Michael Harold Jones is here." He rose. "I need to talk to that guy."

"Go ahead. We're finished here." Mitch stood and held

out his hand again. "Take care, Dr. Shaw. You're in good hands with Grayson watching over you."

"Thanks." She wondered how well Mitch knew Grayson, but there was no time to ask questions. She followed Grayson out of the interview room, intending to return to her usual spot, but Grayson caught her arm.

"I'd like you to watch the interview, see if anything about this guy is familiar," he said in a low voice.

"Of course." She hoped he wasn't pinning his hopes on her meager abilities. "I'll do my best."

He flashed a smile. "I know you will. This way." He led her to the other side of the room where there was another interview room. She could see through the window at the man sitting inside. "He can't see you," Grayson assured her.

She nodded in understanding, knowing she'd never look at cop shows the same way. Not that she watched a lot of television, normally she was too tired mentally to do anything but head to bed.

Grayson left her standing beside Rhy Finnegan to join Joe Kingsley in the interview room. She twisted her hands together and tried to concentrate.

Voices came through the speaker. "I'm Officer Clark, and this is Lieutenant Kingsley," Grayson said. "You are Michael Harold Jones?"

"I go by Mike, yeah." The activist glanced around nervously. "Why am I here?"

"What do you do for a living?" Grayson asked, ignoring the question.

"I'm a software designer for Designs, Inc. Why, is that a crime?" Mike's tone was defensive.

"Are you familiar with the Milwaukee College of Medicine Research Institute?" Grayson asked.

Now Mike fidgeted in his chair. "Yeah. So what if I am? I didn't break any laws."

"You admit you were there two weeks and three days ago, protesting against the use of animals in research?" Grayson pressed.

"Yeah. And you know what?" Mike slapped his hand on the table. "That's what is truly criminal here. They shouldn't be experimenting on animals."

"I see. You have actually seen animals being used for experiments?" Grayson asked.

"Well, no, that's all done in their big secret labs, right?" Mike threw up his hands. "Is that what this is about? Some stupid protest?"

"Tell us about what happened a year ago, when you were charged with breaking and entering and property damage," Grayson went on.

Now Mike flushed. "That was a big misunderstanding," he muttered.

"Why don't you tell us your side of the story?" Joe pressed.

Mike shifted again. "We got bad intel. We were told this guy had several dogs he was using for dog fights. So we broke into his house and freed the animals." He glanced between the two officers. "We only learned later that they weren't being used in illegal dog fights. Like I said, we got bad intel."

Eve could tell Grayson was annoyed with the guy's response. "Did it ever occur to you to double-check your intel before breaking the law?"

Mike shrugged. "I paid the fine and restitution for the damages."

"Did you ever consider the possibility that the research

institute isn't using animals for their research?" Grayson asked. "Maybe you got more bad intel on that topic too."

"They're not going to tell anyone about their secret lab," Mike protested. "Or there would be animal rights groups showing up on their doorstep from all across the country. We're all on this mission together."

No way is this guy the bomber, Eve thought with a sigh. He sounded like an idiot, even though she did agree with his goal to protect animals. Eve wanted to storm inside to assure him there were no secret labs of animals anywhere within the research institute. And that she loved animals as much as he did.

"Where were you last night and early this morning?" Grayson asked.

"I work until five, then I went home. I was with my girlfriend, Amy, all night. I didn't leave my house to go to work this morning until seven fifteen." Understanding dawned. "Oh, this is about that bomb, isn't it? You can't seriously believe I had anything to do with that?"

"Amy, that's Amy Shuller, also a member of the animal rights group?" Grayson asked.

"Yes, that's right. We met at a rally." Mike leaned forward now, his gaze imploring. "I had nothing to do with that bomb. I swear!"

Again, Grayson and Joe exchanged a long look. They asked a few more questions before bringing the interview to a close.

Eve turned away, battling a wave of despair. They were no closer to finding the person responsible than they were earlier this morning.

At this rate, they wouldn't find him until it was too late.

GRAYSON COULDN'T IMAGINE Mike Jones planting bombs, but his background as a software designer indicated he was familiar with computer technology and could have easily tracked Eve's computer to the American Lodge.

Maybe he was one of the fringe players, not the one setting bombs or pulling the trigger of a gun but helping from the background. Too bad, they didn't have anything that could be used as evidence to place him under arrest. With reluctance, they let him go.

"What do you think?" Joe asked, once Jones had left the building.

"He could be a part of this, but he's not the main guy." Grayson shrugged. "I only went through the first five names Gabe gave me. There are more to investigate."

"I have to agree. The group in general seems disorganized." Joe shook his head. "Bad intel? Really?"

"I know. Sloppy at best." He glanced around for Eve. She was back in her usual spot; only this time, her head was down, and she looked completely defeated. His heart squeezed in his chest. He felt bad for putting her through this.

"You better check on her." Joe jutted his chin toward Eve. "But be careful. Don't get in over your head."

"Sure, just like you and Elly," Grayson joked, then sobered. "I know, trust me, I don't want to mess this up."

"God is watching over you, Grayson. Eve too." Joe slapped him on the back. "I know you'll protect her with your life."

"Absolutely." He and the rest of the team, every officer on the force really, put their lives on the line to protect the public every day. But acting as Eve's self-imposed bodyguard was different.

Because she was different. A friend. A high school classmate.

No, if this was one of the guys from his high school football team, he wouldn't be nearly as emotionally invested. If he were being honest with himself, he'd admit his gut was in a knot over his attraction to Eve. He was falling into the same trap as his fellow officers. Joe, Brock, Raelyn, and Steele had all been in a similar position and not all that long ago either.

Too bad, he told himself harshly. *Time to get over it.* He did not want a repeat of what happened with his last girlfriend, Monica.

As if to prove himself immune to her charms, he walked away from Eve toward Gabe Melrose's office. The guy wasn't there, and by the looks of the dark computer, Gabe had obviously left for the day.

He quickly checked his email on his phone, relaxing when he saw he had another email from Melrose with the names and dates of birth for the rest of the people pictured in the animal rights photo.

It would have to be good enough for now. Frankly, he was grateful to have something constructive to do.

He turned to head back to Eve. She looked up as he approached. "May we please leave?"

"Yeah. Sorry about the delay." He pulled the Jeep key fob from his pocket. "Are you okay?"

"Mike didn't set those bombs or try to shoot at me." She sounded deflated. "He's not smart enough and doesn't strike me as someone who is capable of killing in cold blood."

"I agree with your assessment." He tried to gauge where she was coming from. Did she see this as a waste of time? "However, we wouldn't know that without talking to him face-to-face."

She shrugged. "That's true." She abruptly frowned. "Is this what police work is like? Following up on various clues and suspects until you find something useful?"

"Pretty much." He smiled. "It's not glamorous or nonstop action. We tend to pay attention to every single detail. It's often something small that breaks a case wide open."

"That's similar to my work," she confided. "Sifting through details and possibilities like sand on the shores of the ocean until finally discovering something important."

"Exactly." He rested his hand on her back. "I'm sorry that you've had to go through all of this. Did Mike Jones look at all familiar to you? Do you remember seeing him outside the research institute that day?"

"He looks vaguely familiar, yes, but I could not swear he was there the day of the protest. Unfortunately, I didn't pay much attention to any of them at the time. I knew we weren't using animals in our research, so I didn't really bother with them."

"You heard what he said about bad intel?" Grayson asked. "That's the concern I have about these groups. Not that they aren't doing good work in general, but that they don't have their facts straight."

"I heard." She shook her head. "I don't know where the rumor of a secret lab with animals came from. We don't have one."

"Who knows?" He gestured toward the door. "Let's get out of here. I'm hungry."

"Me too," she admitted, then paused. "Do you mind if I stop in the restroom first?"

"Go ahead." He showed her where they were located. "I'll start the car so the air-conditioning is revved up and ready to go."

"Thanks." She ducked inside.

"You're still here?" Rhy came out of his office, heading toward him.

"We're leaving." He grimaced. "Sorry Jones didn't pan out as a viable lead."

"Like you said, he could be involved peripherally. But he looked really shocked to be considered a suspect for the bombing." Rhy glanced at his watch. "I need to hit the road, Devon is waiting for me, and Colleen always greets me as if she hasn't seen me in months." Rhy grinned. "She's kind of like a puppy that way. Now that I think about it, she scoots around on her hands and knees like one too."

He chuckled at the image. And for the first time in his life, he found himself wondering what it would be like to have a wife and daughter waiting for you at home. Parenthood wasn't something he'd thought about much, especially after Monica, until Rhy and Devon had Colleen. Their daughter was seven months old now, and there was a rumor going around that Rhy and Devon were already planning baby number two.

Considering Tarin's wife, Joy, had given birth to a baby boy a few months ago, and Kyleigh had recently delivered a baby girl, the Finnegan family seemed anxious to populate the world with more Finnegans. Although in Kyleigh's case, she was a Scala, having married ADA Bax Scala.

His parents had waited until he'd gone to college to split up, but he'd always known they weren't happy. He figured that was one of the reasons he'd never been able to find a woman he cared enough about to settle down. That along with the incident with Monica had him shying away from commitment. He didn't think it was fair to bring kids into the world only to end up divorced.

But he'd noticed the Finnegans had not only jumped

into relationships with startling quickness, they rushed to the altar too.

He didn't get it.

"You need anything else?" Rhy asked.

"Nope." He smiled when Eve emerged from the restroom. "We'll walk out with you."

"Sure thing." Rhy waited for them to catch up. Together, they headed for the side door. Grayson took a moment to double click the key fob to start the Jeep.

The sun was still warm, but there was a cool breeze coming in from the west. He figured it wouldn't take long for the air-conditioning to kick in.

He and Eve had just joined Rhy when the Jeep exploded, the blast knocking them off their feet.

"Eve!" he shouted, searching for her. Had she been hit?

"Here." Her voice was hoarse. "I'm here."

Thank You, Lord! Even as the prayer formed in his mind, he stared dumbly at the wreckage.

Someone had planted another bomb. But who had known they would be here at the precinct at this time? Mike Jones had been brought in for questioning, but he couldn't know that Grayson would be the one to talk to him.

Possibilities swirled in his mind as Rhy called 911 to report the blast. The only thing he knew with grim certainty is that if he hadn't used the remote start, he and Eve would both be dead.

CHAPTER SIX

Another bomb! Eve stared at what was left of the Jeep in horror. Even a police station parking lot wasn't safe.

"Get back inside," Rhy said in a tense tone that she could barely hear beyond the ringing in her ears. "Hurry."

When she didn't move fast enough, Grayson took her arm and helped her up. "Let's go, Eve."

The bomb was meant for her and would have killed Grayson too. The thought brought a flash of anger. Enough was enough! This violence had to stop!

"You need to let me go somewhere on my own," she told Grayson as they sought shelter inside the precinct. "Give me a vehicle to use and I'll disappear for a while."

"What are you talking about?" Grayson didn't release her arm. "Going off alone is only asking for trouble."

"I'm supposed to let them kill you too?" She tried to tug her arm from him but couldn't. She couldn't hide her desperation. "And what about other innocent people who could be harmed because they happen to be standing close to me? I can't be responsible for that, Grayson. I just can't."

"This isn't your fault." He tugged her close, putting his

arm around her shoulders. "I promise we'll get to the bottom of these attacks. And I will do everything in my power to keep you safe."

She shook her head, unwilling to accept that. "I would rather go somewhere by myself. I'll stay off the internet; I won't do any research. No one will know where I am." *Even you*, she silently added.

"I'm not leaving you." Grayson's dark eyes bored into hers. "We don't know how we were found here. Maybe this perp was able to track your phone."

Her phone? A shiver rippled down her spine. "I never thought of that. It's paid for by the research institute."

"Give it to me." Rhy held out his hand. "I'll get rid of it."

She dug in her oversized bag for the device and handed it over. He shut it down, then dropped it on the floor and crushed it beneath his heel.

"I called Zeke. He has a spare vehicle you can use for a few days," Rhy said as he tossed her damaged phone in the closest garbage can.

"The old Ford sedan?" Grayson wrinkled his nose and shook his head. "That's nice of him to offer, but I'd rather have something more reliable."

"Zeke said he'd use the sedan, so you can borrow his truck." Rhy's expression was serious. "I've asked Gabe to log in from home to check the security cameras too. Maybe he'll get a decent photo of the bomber."

She brightened at that.

"I shouldn't have parked the Jeep along the back row," Grayson said. "It never occurred to me that someone would find it and plant a bomb."

Rhy sighed. "I don't think we'll be able to repair the Jeep this time. It's gone for good, and Michaels will have a fit." He shook his head. "I don't like this, Grayson. Maybe the cell phone was tracked, or maybe the word went out that we picked up Jones for an interview."

It took a moment for her to follow his train of thought. "You believe the animal rights group is involved? That they knew you were speaking with Michael Harold Jones and came out here to plant the bomb?" It made sense to a point. "Okay, say they did manage to pull that off. How could they have discovered we were using the Jeep? That was hardly common knowledge to anyone outside the precinct."

"That's a good question. I don't have all the answers, but I'm not ruling anything out. I don't like coincidences." Rhy gestured toward one of the desks. "Have a seat. I need to make a few calls."

She sank into the closest chair, her mind whirling. It dawned on her that if this bomber had the ability to track her phone, they could have been found at the City Central Hotel.

She wondered if she'd ever be safe. Then she felt ashamed of the depressing thought. Enough wallowing in self-pity. She needed to be grateful that God had been watching over them.

She closed her eyes. *Thank You, Lord. Please continue to keep Grayson and the others safe in Your care. Amen.*

"Eve? Please don't go off on your own," Grayson said in a low voice.

She looked at him and reluctantly nodded. "I won't, but I still don't like exposing you and the others to danger."

"Protecting the public is our job," he said. "That's what the city pays me to do."

She sighed. "I know that, but I care about you, Grayson. I don't want anything to happen to you or the other members of your team. Rhy has a wife and a baby. What if he'd been hurt or killed?"

"I feel the same way about you and Rhy too." He reached for her hand. "We have leads to follow, so don't give up hope yet."

"I haven't given up hope. We have been blessed by God watching over us. Shielding us from danger."

Grayson nodded slowly. "You may be right about that."

It warmed her heart to hear him speak of faith. Yet their situation was still troubling. Before she could say anything more, Rhy returned.

"Gabe is looking at the camera, but it looks like the front of the Jeep may be out of range." He grimaced. "He's going to see if there are any other businesses nearby that have cameras pointing toward the parking lot."

Nothing on the cameras? She swallowed her disappointment.

"Zeke and Jina are on their way in two cars so they can leave the truck here for you to use." Rhy rubbed the back of his neck. "I have the rest of the team heading over to sweep the area surrounding the police station to make sure there aren't other devices nearby."

She caught her breath. More devices? She remembered how Grayson had checked her bright-blue SUV in the parking lot of the research institute and wondered how long something like that would take.

"You can't go back to the City Central Hotel," Rhy continued. "I arranged for a room at the Timberland Falls Suites. The reservation is under the MPD account, so hopefully that will offer enough protection for you."

"Michaels approved it?" Grayson asked, sounding surprised.

"The Jeep blew up here in our parking lot, so yeah, he didn't argue." Rhy scowled. "We need to get this guy and soon."

"We will." Grayson sounded confident. "Thanks for arranging the room. We'll head there as soon as Zeke and Jina arrive."

"They're going to call when they get here and meet you outside the main entrance." Rhy glanced toward the side door. "I need to speak with the team and Mitch Callahan. We know these attempts are connected, and I'm hoping Mitch can gather enough information on the devices to prove it."

"Be careful," she said, not hiding her concern.

Rhy's smile was brief. "Don't worry. I have a feeling this guy is long gone. The device was triggered by Grayson using the key fob to start the Jeep's engine. If our perp planned to detonate the device via some sort of remote control, he would have waited for you and Grayson to get inside."

Her eyes widened in horror. His theory was hardly reassuring.

"Go, Rhy. Then head home to your family." Grayson looked at Rhy with concern. "I'm glad you're okay."

"You and Eve too." Rhy gave a small nod, then headed outside through the side door. "Call me if anything changes."

"Always," Grayson promised. There was a long silence after Rhy left before he spoke again. "I feel like I should be out there helping," Grayson said.

She tightened her grip on his hand, hoping he wouldn't leave. "I'm glad you're here. And that you're safe."

"Ditto," he murmured. Then he released her to check his phone. She realized he'd gotten an incoming text. "Zeke and Jina will be here in five minutes."

"Okay." She glanced around the police station, which

was unusually quiet. "I hope they don't find any more devices."

"I don't think they will. This guy is fixated on you." Grayson frowned when his gaze landed on her bag. "I guess it's a good thing you brought your computer and notes with you. I'll need to grab another laptop."

She nodded, realizing he was right. Thank goodness she hadn't lost her notes. The delay in her ability to work was bad enough.

And that only made her realize again how important it was to find this guy as soon as possible. With every delay, thousands of people's lives continued to be ruled by their disease, checking their blood sugar and injecting themselves with insulin or taking other medications every single day.

Deep down, she knew her mother's disease had spiraled out of control in part due to her lack of compliance. But even those who were really good about keeping track of their numbers suffered detrimental side effects of their high blood sugar. By the time her mother had died, she was almost completely blind and suffered severe neuropathy in her feet.

She hoped this new technique she was working on to rejuvenate the pancreatic hormonal secretion cells would work. The pancreas was a gland, like the thyroid, pituitary, and adrenal glands, among others. The impact of her research was potentially far-reaching, beyond just treating diabetes. There were other diseases that may also be able to be cured.

It was extremely difficult to sit back doing nothing while Grayson and the rest of the team searched for the man responsible for these attacks. And as Grayson had pointed out, that may be the goal. One she did not understand.

"They're here," Grayson said, breaking into her

thoughts. He had a laptop case slung over his shoulder, a replacement for the one he'd left at the City Central Hotel.

She rose to her feet and lifted her bag onto her shoulder. "Maybe I should place my notes in a safe deposit box," she said, mostly to herself. "At least then I'd know they would be safe from harm."

"That's not the worst idea, but we can't do that until morning." Grayson rested his hand on the small of her back. "I'm going to head outside first. I want you to stay behind me."

"I understand." She didn't like it but knew arguing was useless. Grayson would protect her no matter what.

She couldn't see beyond Grayson's broad shoulders as they left the building. She heard him call out, "Hey, Zeke. Thanks for the ride. I owe you one."

"Nah, we're all in this together," a male voice responded. "I can't believe the Jeep was blown to bits."

"Yeah, thankfully without us being inside." Grayson reached the sidewalk, then opened the door to a black truck. "Slide in, Eve."

She did so, placing her bag on the floor first, before scrambling inside. Zeke eyed her curiously but then tossed the keys to Grayson. "Try not to get my truck blown up."

"That's the goal," Grayson said. He waved at Jina, a beautiful blonde who sat behind the wheel of a four-door sedan. "Take care and I'll be in touch."

"You got it. We're heading out back to help sweep the area." Zeke nodded at Jina. "It's not likely we'll find anything, but you know Rhy wants us to be sure. Based on how close this one hit to home, I don't blame him."

"I hear you." Grayson slid in behind the wheel. "Good luck."

She buckled herself in as Grayson pulled away from the

curb. She tried not to show her nerves as he headed toward the interstate. "Timberland Falls is outside your jurisdiction, isn't it?"

"That's true." He shrugged. "Although our team has been called in to help support the suburbs of Milwaukee and the eastern part of Waukesha because of our close proximity." He reached over to squeeze her hand. "We'll be safe in Timberland Falls. We have to make a stop along the way, though, to pick up replacement phones."

"Okay." She didn't much care about the phone, and there was no point in telling him she didn't feel safe anywhere. That was her problem, not his. The man who had targeted her was flesh and blood, not someone with superhuman powers. People made mistakes.

And she firmly believed Grayson would find him.

It was only a matter of time.

And she could only pray that it would happen sooner rather than later.

HIS STOMACH WAS RUMBLING LOUDLY by the time they reached the Timberland Falls Suites. Picking up disposable phones was quick and painless. Eve had seemed interested in the way they worked, having never used one before. He explained the technology along the way.

Their room was ready, and it didn't take long for them to get settled inside. He preferred having a suite rather than using connecting rooms. They would still have privacy while sharing a central living space. He grabbed the room service menu, hoping it wouldn't take too long for the food to be delivered.

"Lots of options here." He scanned the menu, decided

on a cheeseburger, and handed it to Eve. "Let me know what you'd like. There are soft drinks too."

"I'll have the grilled chicken and water. I don't like all the chemicals in soft drinks." She sighed and rubbed her eyes. "I don't know why, but it seems wrong to be hungry at a time like this."

"It's not wrong." He frowned. "Our bodies need fuel to fight this attacker. It's important that we stay hydrated too." He reached for the phone and placed their order, opting for water as well. He'd never worried about the chemicals in soft drinks before, but if Eve said they were a problem, he was inclined to believe her.

That was her field of expertise after all.

He quickly placed the computer on the table and booted it up, then took a few minutes to deal with the new phones. When they were charging up, he turned back to the computer. He needed to start looking into the names Gabe had provided for the rest of the people who were in the animal rights group photo. If Mike Jones was the tech guy who somehow traced Eve by her computer and her phone, one of the others was likely the bomber.

Even one of the women, he reminded himself. He'd been a cop long enough to know that gender didn't mean much when it came to committing crimes.

Then again, he could be on the wrong path altogether. Jones didn't come across as overly bright and capable of doing something like this.

He was working through the second name when a knock at the door startled him. He was so intent on his work that he'd almost forgotten about the food. He closed the laptop, shot to his feet, and double-checked through the peephole before opening the door.

"Thanks." He gave the server a tip, then took the tray. "Eve, will you take a moment to lock the door?"

"Sure." She did so, then joined him at the table. "Smells great."

"I know, please excuse any drool," he joked. He uncovered the plates and sat down, then belatedly remembered Eve would want to pray.

She glanced at him, then seemed to realize he was waiting for her. "Dear Lord Jesus, we thank You for this wonderful food you've provided for us. We ask that You continue to keep us all safe in Your care, especially Grayson and the members of the tactical team. Amen."

"Amen." He was touched by her sweet prayer. "Thanks for including the team."

"Of course. I wouldn't be here if not for you and the others." Her brow furrowed as she picked up a french fry. "I still can't believe someone is trying to kill me."

He could understand that. As a cop, he was used to being hated on principal, thanks to the handful of bad apples. Yet he could say with certainty that he didn't know of anyone who hated him on a personal level.

Even Monica hadn't hated him. Just the opposite. He quickly pushed that memory aside.

Taking a big bite of his cheeseburger, he focused on the two names he'd managed to investigate so far. What else could he do if he made it through the entire list and still had nothing to go on? They needed something. Anything to break this case open.

Hopefully, Mitch Callahan would come through on the bomb fragments. It was sometimes possible to get fingerprints off them, but he wasn't going to bank on that. From what he saw beneath Eve's desk, it was a basic pipe bomb with a trigger device. That particular bomb had been built with C4, but he had no way of knowing if they all were built the same.

And what about the gunman at the American Lodge? That seemed to be an aberration from the killer's MO.

"Grayson?" He glanced at Eve. "Do you think a police officer could be involved?"

"What? No way." He was surprised she'd mentioned that possibility. "Why would a cop care about your research?"

"No reason, it just seems strange to plant a bomb outside a police station. And that he managed to escape being caught on the security cameras." She flushed and shrugged. "Ignore me, I wouldn't make a very good cop."

"No, you're right to ask those types of questions." He couldn't blame her for being suspicious. "I can't imagine any cop wanting to stop your research, but I promise to keep my mind open to all possibilities, okay?"

She nodded and took another bite of her sandwich. They ate in silence for long moments. He wanted to reassure her everything would work out fine, but so far, they'd barely escaped with their lives, not once but several times.

He couldn't help but think Rhy, Joe, and the other believers on the team were right about how God was protecting them.

Even Raelyn had gotten engaged to Pastor Isaiah Washington last week. If anyone had predicted something like that, he'd have laughed in their face.

When they'd finished eating, he placed their dirty dishes on the tray and set it in the hallway outside their door. Time to get back to work.

Eve wandered around the suite, obviously unable to settle down. After a few minutes, he glanced at her. "You can watch something on television if you'd like. It won't bother me."

Her cheeks went pink. "I so rarely watch TV I have no idea what's on these days."

"Use the TV guide function. I'm sure you'll find something familiar."

"No thanks." She returned to the sofa and dug in her bag for her endless supply of sticky notes.

It took him an hour to get through the list, and all he had to show for it was a woman named Marlene who had a minor assault and battery charge. Rather than bothering Gabe Melrose for the police report, he did a search on her name and found an article in a local paper. Turned out, her assault and battery charge was related to hitting a pedestrian on the head with her sign, which resulted in the pedestrian getting a couple of stitches.

"That's it," he said with a sigh of disappointment. "I didn't find anything else that would indicate the group is responsible."

"Maybe they are but so far have managed to avoid being caught," she said.

"Yeah." It was the same argument he'd used earlier, but in truth, criminals didn't just wake up one day and decide to set bombs to blow people up. Normally those prone to violence had other brushes with the law.

He scrubbed his hands over his face. It wasn't that late, but the long day was catching up to him. Glancing at Eve, he noticed she was yawning too.

"We should get some sleep." He closed the computer and stood. "Things will look better in the morning."

"You think so?" She frowned, clearly doubting him. "Would Rhy or the others call you if they found something?"

"They would, but I'll check in if that makes you feel better." He thumbed his phone to find Zeke's number. His teammate answered on the second ring. "Hey, how did the search go?"

"We didn't find anything, so Joe called it a night," Zeke said. "Mitch Callahan was there, too, but he said he couldn't do much with what was left of the Jeep until the morning."

"Yeah, I get it." He masked his disappointment. "I just went through the list of names Gabe sent on the local animal rights group. I didn't find anything to work with."

"That reminds me, Mitch was asking about Eve's former boyfriend," Zeke said. "Some guy who works in the hospital, right?"

"That's right. Andrew Thomas. Joe ran him through the system, but nothing popped from a criminal perspective." He glanced at Eve, who was listening to his side of the conversation with interest. "Why did Mitch ask about him?"

"He mentioned stopping by the guy's condo, but he wasn't there. Sounds like Mitch wants to interview the guy."

"I'd like to be there for that," Grayson said.

"Talk to Rhy and Joe," Zeke suggested. "I'm just filling you in on the conversation outside the precinct."

"I will. Anything else?" Grayson asked.

"Just that there was a body found at the research institute," Zeke said. "Mitch said the person was buried under some heavy lab equipment, so they didn't find her right away."

Her? He glanced cautiously at Eve, knowing this would hit her hard. "Do you have an ID?"

"Yeah, hang on a minute." There was a brief pause as

Zeke searched for the information. "Pauline Klug. My understanding is that she's a lab tech of some sort."

"Okay, thanks for letting me know. Get some sleep, we'll talk more tomorrow." Grayson lowered the phone.

"What is it?" Eve stepped closer, searching his gaze. "I can tell by the look on your face something is wrong."

"You might want to sit down." He couldn't lie to her even though he'd rather wait until morning to give her this latest news.

"Who died?" She sat on the edge of the sofa.

He nodded slowly, sinking down beside her. "Do you know a lab tech by the name of Pauline Klug?"

She sucked in a harsh breath. "Yes. Pauline is a very skilled tech. Was she hurt in the blast?"

"She's dead, Eve." He reached for her hand. "I'm sorry, but they didn't find her body right away because it was buried under some heavy equipment."

She gripped his hand tightly and bowed her head. "Pauline didn't deserve this."

"No. And neither do you." He scooted closer so he could wrap his arm around her shoulders. Eve abruptly turned toward him, burying her face against his chest.

He held her as her slender shoulders shook with her sobs, her tears soaking his shirt. He gathered her closer still, wishing he could think of something that would offer her some measure of comfort.

But words of wisdom failed him. Selfishly, his main thought was to be grateful that Eve's life was spared.

Thank You, Lord, he silently whispered, cradling her in his arms. *Thank You!*

CHAPTER SEVEN

Eve pulled herself together with an effort. Crying on Grayson's shoulder wouldn't change anything. And it certainly wouldn't bring Pauline back. Her church pastor would say that Pauline was in a better place, and while she shared that belief, it was still difficult to know the poor woman had died because some maniac had targeted Eve.

Because of her research? That truly didn't make any sense.

"Sorry," she murmured, lifting her head from the warm comfort of his chest and swiping at her eyes. "I didn't mean to fall apart like that."

"You can fall apart on me any time." He lifted his hand and tucked a strand of her hair behind her ear. "I'm here for you, Eve."

"I know." She tried to smile, but her face felt stiff. "It's so maddening to know an innocent woman was killed because someone is holding a grudge against me."

"It could be that the bomber assumed the lab would be empty."

She scowled. "That doesn't make it right. You don't

blow up an office without considering innocent lives may be in danger."

"You're right." He hugged her close and pressed a kiss to her temple. It was all she could do not to throw herself back into his arms. "I promise to keep pushing forward with the investigation to uncover who is behind this."

"I know you will." She injected confidence into her tone. Right now, she needed to believe Grayson and the rest of the team would find the person responsible and soon.

Before he could strike again.

He hugged her again, and she relaxed into his arms. What was the point of fighting her feelings? Maybe this was nothing more than a brief interlude for Grayson—despite how he claimed he wasn't seeing anyone as she was sure he had plenty of women to choose from—but she needed this.

Needed him.

She'd been looking for comfort, yet now there was a definite attraction humming between them. More so on her part, she knew. She snaked her arms around his waist and hugged him hard, wishing for more.

"Eve." His voice was a husky whisper near her ear. "You should probably try to get some sleep."

Was that his way of telling her to let go? With a soundless sigh, she released her grip and lifted her head. "I'm sure you're exhausted too."

He nodded, his gaze clinging to hers. Was it her imagination, or was he going to kiss her?

She was convinced she moved first, leaning in to meet him halfway. His mouth captured hers, sending a sizzle of heat shooting through her.

In high school, she'd imagined kissing him, but even her best attempt didn't match reality. He gathered her close, deepening their kiss.

She kissed him back, but suddenly he was breaking off their embrace and taking deep breaths. "I—uh, we can't do this."

Why not? She almost said the words out loud. Instead, she managed to nod. "Oh, um, okay."

He let out a low groan and shook his head. "Kissing you was something I'd wanted to do back in high school, but I need to stay focused on the danger." His expression sobered. "I can't afford to lower my guard. I hope you understand."

In truth, she had no idea what he was talking about. He'd wanted to kiss her back in high school? But then again, emotions and feelings were not her strong suit. "I do. It's fine." She leaned back and glanced around the suite as if seeing it for the first time. "Which room is mine?"

"Take your pick." He didn't move from his spot on the sofa as she stood and glanced at the two bedroom doors.

She took the one on her right for no good reason other than it was closer. "Good night, Grayson."

"Good night."

She felt his gaze boring into her back as she made her way across the room. Then she frowned when she remembered she'd left her small suitcase at the City Central Hotel. Oh well, it wasn't like Grayson had a change of clothes or toiletries either.

No complaining, she lectured herself as she closed the bedroom door behind her. After everything they'd been through, she was grateful to be alive.

She lifted her fingers to lips that still tingled from Grayson's kiss. No wonder he had cheerleaders falling all over him in high school. The man could kiss.

Or maybe her experiences with men were just that lame.

She'd walked in to find Andrew kissing a beautiful blond woman dressed in a short skirt and formfitting blouse and three-inch-high heels. Andrew had claimed Bambi—seriously, who named their kid Bambi?—was a close friend, but she knew better. For one thing, Andrew had kissed Bambi with more passion than he'd ever shown her, and besides, she recognized the woman as a pharmaceutical sales representative for Owens and Powers Pharmaceuticals. One of the up-and-coming drug companies to cash in on the sales of prescription medications.

She didn't doubt that Andrew, who had the authority to prescribe diabetes medications, had gladly used some of O&P's newest diabetes drugs, despite the fact that they were more costly than those that had been on the market for years. And that was due to the infamous Bambi.

Whatever. It didn't matter. Andrew was old news. She and Grayson had bigger issues to worry about. She needed Grayson to find the person responsible for the bombings so that she could return to her research.

Earlier, she'd tried to recover the notes she'd lost in her office, but her mind had not been able to recreate a single one.

What if those notes were gone forever? No, she couldn't allow herself to think the worst. Once she was back at her desk, working through her experimental data, the ideas she'd jotted down would return.

Pushing away from the door, she washed up, then climbed into bed. Maybe her subconscious would help to recreate some of those lost notes.

Instead, her mind replayed those wonderfully intense and sizzling moments of Grayson's kiss.

At some point she must have fallen asleep because the next thing she knew, light was streaming in through the window. She blinked, then nearly groaned when she saw the time was barely six o'clock in the morning.

She knew from past experience that falling back asleep wouldn't happen, so she dragged herself up and splashed cold water on her face. Unfortunately, she couldn't wash her hair without a hairbrush, so she raked her fingers through the dull brown strands trying to get rid of her bedhead.

It didn't work.

Muttering under her breath, she made the bed, then followed the enticing scent of coffee. Of course, Grayson was up, dressed, and even with his five o'clock shadow looked as if he'd just stepped off the cover of *GQ*.

Men. They had it so easy, she thought crossly.

"Good morning. How did you sleep?" His cheery attitude wasn't helping. Was he always like this in the morning?

"Fine." She headed straight for the coffee. After taking a bracing sip, she turned to face him. "I don't suppose you have any updates on the case?"

"Not yet. But I would like to interview your ex-boyfriend first thing."

She frowned at him over the rim of her cup. "I thought you said he wasn't home when they stopped in?"

"He wasn't, but I'm sure he was working, right?" He grinned. "With your help, we can track him down in the hospital."

"We can't go traipsing through the hospital intruding on sick people," she protested. "That's not fair to them. Besides, all visitors have to check in at the front desk to let the security guards know who they intend to visit."

"Figures they finally tightened up their security," he grumbled. "I really want to talk to him, Eve. And I need your input on how he responds. You know him better than we do and can probably tell if he's lying."

"Not sure about that, but okay. I get your point." She glanced at the clock. "Andrew starts at eight. We should be able to catch him in the doctor's parking structure."

"Or better yet, at his home prior to him leaving for work," Grayson countered. "Come on. We need to talk to him."

She stifled a sigh. It was too early for this. "Fine. But he probably leaves by seven thirty, so we'll have to head out soon."

"Perfect. We'll grab a bite to eat afterward." He looked pleased with having gotten his way.

"Can I finish my coffee first?" She was trying hard not to sound as cranky as she felt. One cup didn't seem too much to ask.

"Bring it along." He clearly was eager to go. "I don't want to risk missing him."

She stared at him for a long moment, then nodded. "Fine. He lives in a condo in Brookland that isn't too far from Trinity Medical Center."

"Great. It should only take fifteen to twenty minutes to get there." He dug in his pocket for Zeke's truck keys and moved toward the door.

"Wait. I want to take my bag." She set her coffee aside, then gathered her notes together and stuffed them back in her oversized bag. This trip probably wouldn't be dangerous, but after everything she'd experienced so far, she wasn't leaving her notes behind.

"Okay, you have a point. I'll grab the laptop too." Grayson moved toward the table to pack up the device.

A few minutes later, she followed him out of the suite. At some level, she dreaded knocking on Andrew's door this early since it was doubtful he'd be alone. Either Bambi or some other woman would likely be there too.

Telling herself it didn't matter, she set her bag on the floor of the passenger seat and hopped into the truck. She hadn't brought her coffee, knowing she'd only end up spilling it down her front. Grayson had mentioned getting breakfast, so she'd have to settle for that.

"Do you need directions?" she asked, after Grayson stashed his computer behind his seat and slid in behind the wheel. "It's a side-by-side condo complex near Bishop's Woods. It's right off the interstate."

"A side by side? Not a three-story building near the Irish Pub?"

"Not that one," she confirmed. "It's a few miles from there. Did you used to live in the three-story building?"

"Not me but Alanna Finnegan, or rather Alanna Carmichael used to live there." He flashed a smile. "Rhy is the oldest of nine kids. Alanna is second youngest of the clan."

"Wow." She couldn't imagine that. "I was an only child."

"I have an older brother, Lincoln, but he's currently living in Los Angeles. He's married with two kids and works for one of the giant tech firms."

She hadn't known that about him. "Do you get to see your brother's family often?"

"Not really." Grayson's smile faded. "Our parents divorced when we were just starting college. Lincoln tended to take Dad's side, while I was closer to Mom."

She reached over to rest her hand on his arm. "I'm sorry. That sounds complicated."

"That's one way to describe it." Grayson shrugged. "It doesn't matter. Lincoln is a nice guy, and we don't harbor ill feelings or anything. We just don't have a lot in common. I didn't have a very high opinion of marriage in general until Rhy and his family started getting married. I admit, they are the real deal."

"My parents were too." She had known her parents had loved each other; their mutual support and caring was obvious. She'd assumed she'd find someone who loved her the same way, but that hadn't happened.

She wondered if Grayson's jaded view of relationships had kept him single for this long.

Then she reminded herself that his personal life wasn't her concern. The moment they had the bomber behind bars, they'd both go their separate ways.

By the time they reached Andrew's condo complex, she was wishing she had risked bringing the coffee. The car ride made her sleepy.

"Do you know which one?" he asked as they drove up to the cluster of side-by-side condos.

"Yes. The second from the right." She gestured through the window.

Grayson parked on the road in front of the condo. She slid out of her seat and walked up toward the front door. Grayson quickly joined her.

"Follow my lead on this," he said as he rapped on the door.

"What does that mean?" She frowned. "I thought you wanted me here to let you know if I think he's lying?"

"That and maybe you'll think of questions to ask him that I've missed." He waited a few minutes, then knocked again.

She nodded, straining to listen. There were no sounds coming from inside. She frowned, wondering if Andrew had gone into work early.

"Is he a sound sleeper?" Grayson asked.

"How would I know?" She stared at him. "We didn't sleep together."

"Okay, I just thought I'd ask." Grayson knocked again, then leaned on the doorbell. Even from outside, she could hear it, the sound of the doorbell reverberating through the interior of the condo.

Still nothing. Maybe Andrew was a sound sleeper. Or maybe he was with someone tucked away in bed. She had always suspected her refusal to spend the night with him was part of the reason he'd found someone else. Even if she was a bimbo like Bambi.

"Maybe we should see if his car is still in the garage," Grayson said. "We could have missed him."

"Maybe." She moved off the front porch to look through the front window. At first, she didn't see anything.

Then she saw a bare foot poking out from behind the breakfast bar as if the person was lying on the floor. A cold chill washed over her. "Grayson? Look!" She pointed to the foot.

Had something bad happened to Andrew?

THE BARE FOOT sticking out from behind the counter was not good. Pulling his phone, he called Rhy, knowing his boss lived in Brookland and was only minutes away.

"What's going on?" Rhy asked. In the background, he could hear babbling from baby Colleen.

"We're at Andrew Thomas's condo in Brookland, and someone is lying on the floor. I'm going to break in under exigent circumstances."

"Go ahead. Call 911 and I'll meet you there. What's the address again?"

Grayson rattled it off. Then he turned to Eve. "Call 911. I'm going in." Without waiting for her to respond, he went up and examined the doorframe. It looked sturdy, but he kicked it once, twice, and a third time, before the doorjamb gave way beneath the pressure.

Inside, a horrible stench confirmed what he'd already suspected. Doing his best to breathe through his mouth, he pulled his weapon and entered the condo. "Police! Is anyone here?"

There was no response, not that he expected one. He quickly crossed into the kitchen, looking down at a man lying on the floor wearing nothing but a pair of gym shorts. The back of the guy's head was bloody, likely bashed in with the bloodstained hammer lying on the floor beside the body.

Bending at the knees while taking care not to encroach on the crime scene, he felt for a pulse. The guy's skin was cold to the touch. He was no ME, but clearly Andrew Thomas had been dead for a while.

Overnight at least, maybe longer. He wasn't sure what time Rhy had sent someone here to interview him. But he highly doubted anyone from the team would have missed seeing this bare foot.

The ME would tell them for sure. He stared at the guy for a moment, realizing his torso was twisted a bit, as if maybe he'd turned toward the attacker, but not in enough time. The way the guy had fallen was strange too. A blow to the back of the head would send him staggering forward, but he was lying on his back.

The detail bothered him, but he forced himself to let it go. There were crime scene experts who would be able to recreate the scene of the attack. He backed off from the dead man and quickly cleared the condo before going back outside, checking the windows and the back door from a distance. There was no sign of a forced entry, making him believe the victim had opened his door to let the killer inside. He didn't dig any deeper, though, knowing the crime scene techs would do a better job of that than he would.

He crossed to the broken door and stepped outside, gulping fresh air.

"He's dead, isn't he?" Eve's voice was subdued.

"Yeah." He glanced at her. "I'm sorry. I think he's been there for a while."

"I can't believe this." She looked dazed and confused. "How did this happen? Was he shot? Do you think the same shooter who came after us at the American Lodge came here instead?"

"No, he wasn't shot. Someone hit him on the back of his head with a hammer. And was nice enough to leave the murder weapon behind."

"A hammer? Really?" She frowned and shook her head. "That's odd. I didn't realize he had any woodworking tools. Andrew isn't the type to do home repairs. That's why he bought this condo."

Interesting insight. "The murderer could have brought the hammer with him or her." He noticed Rhy's black SUV already pulling up behind Zeke's truck. "The MO is so different from the bombings; I have to wonder if Andrew's death isn't connected to them."

"A coincidence?" She looked pale in the sunlight. "I don't know about that."

He didn't know either, but hopefully they'd get some answers soon. He took Eve's arm and steered her away from the house. "Hey, Rhy. Andrew Thomas is dead, killed with a blow to the head with a hammer that was left behind. I cleared the house; there was no one lurking inside. I didn't see any obvious signs of a forced entry, but I didn't want to contaminate the crime scene by getting too close." He gestured to the front door. "That is my work, but it was securely locked and took me several tries to break in."

Rhy nodded grimly. "What brought you out here so early?"

He shuffled his feet, knowing Rhy wanted to know why he'd jumped the gun and took action on the case without clearing it with him or Joe first. "I know you were going to send someone to interview him, but I thought it might be better to do that with Eve, since she knew the guy on a personal level."

"I told Grayson that Andrew started work at eight o'clock in the morning, so we thought we'd try to get here before he left the condo," Eve quickly interjected. He was touched at how she stepped up to defend him when she hadn't been that enthusiastic about coming here in the first place. "When Andrew didn't answer the door, I looked through the window and saw his bare foot. Well, to be honest, I didn't know for sure it was his, but it was definitely a man's foot, and I know Andrew dates women."

"Thanks for filling me in, Eve," Rhy said kindly, then turned to Grayson with a knowing look. "You got anything more to tell me?"

"I'm sorry, Cap. It was my idea to talk to him first thing." He knew it was better to take responsibility for his actions. Rhy and Joe were both fair men, but they also had high standards for their team. "Obviously I had no idea we'd find him dead, or I wouldn't have come or brought Eve with me." He cleared his throat. "And the hammer is an interesting choice of weapon. According to Eve, he wasn't much on home repairs."

"I'll make a note for the crime scene techs to search for a tool kit." Rhy blew out his breath. "I don't know what to think. The hammer is a very different MO from the bombs and the gunfire, but the link to Eve is difficult to ignore."

"I agree. It's very strange." Grayson wished he'd have thought of coming here last evening. So much had happened, especially the last bomb that destroyed the Jeep, that he'd thought checking in with Eve's ex could wait until morning.

"Andrew wasn't exactly monogamous." Eve's pale cheeks were now flushed with embarrassment. "I caught him cheating on me with a woman named Bambi. It could be that someone else caught him in the act too."

"Bambi? Is that some sort of nickname?" Grayson asked.

"Not sure, her nametag refers to her as Bambi, so I assumed it was her actual name." Her mouth curved in a wry smile. "She works for O&P."

"What is O&P?" Rhy asked with a frown. "I never heard of it."

"Owens and Powers Pharmaceuticals," Eve said. "They're a relatively new drug company, they came out with a breakthrough diabetes drug that is now a rival for Ozempic and others that can also be used for weight loss as well as diabetes. I assume Bambi was trying to convince Andrew to prescribe her company's new drug when they became romantically involved."

"Maybe this is a personal attack against the guy," Rhy said thoughtfully.

"You're saying Bambi learned Andrew was cheating and bopped him on the head with the hammer?" Saying the words out loud only made them seem more ridiculous.

"I don't know," Eve said with a sigh. "Andrew is not the faithful type. And you know that old saying about a woman scorned. For all I know, he could have had a string of girlfriends like Bambi." She held his gaze for a moment as if comparing him to Andrew. He didn't appreciate that since he'd never dated more than one woman at a time. Monica's face flashed in his mind, and he pushed it away with an effort. "Either way, he didn't deserve to be murdered in his own home."

The ear-splitting sound of sirens grew louder as the 911 responders arrived. He wished he could tell them there was no reason to hurry, but as the ambulance rolled to a stop behind the squad, they seemed to realize they weren't needed.

"I'll talk to them," Rhy said, moving in that direction. "But stick around, Grayson. Brookland PD will want your statement and Eve's too."

"Got it." He reached out to take Eve's hand, waiting until Rhy was out of earshot to say, "I never cheated on my girlfriends. I dated a lot, yes. But one at a time, and most of the time, the end of the relationship was mutual." *Except with Monica*, he thought with a sigh. His big failure.

"That's not how I remember it," she said. "You had a different girlfriend every week."

He wanted to defend himself, then realized they were talking about the way he lived his life ten years ago in high school. He was about to tell her he didn't date women the way he used to when a shout caught his attention.

"Are you Grayson Clark?" a uniformed officer asked. His Brookland PD nametag read Rawson. "Did you move the body?"

"No, I only briefly touched his neck to check for a

carotid pulse." He frowned. "What makes you think the body was moved?"

"Oh, it was definitely rolled over," the cop said. "I'm thinking the murderer rolled him onto his back to make it easier to verify he was dead."

That would explain the twisted torso, he thought. But there were still too many unanswered questions.

Who killed Andrew Thomas, and why? And was the guy's death related to the attempts against Eve?

CHAPTER EIGHT

Andrew was dead. Eve grappled with the news, trying to make sense of it all. She hadn't loved him, but she had cared about him. And even though it made no sense that his murder was related to the attacks against her, she could not shake the cloak of guilt.

Why was this happening? She stood outside Zeke's truck, feeling oddly detached as she watched the police and ambulance crew swarm the area. It felt similar to the way she'd stood outside the research institute. As if this were an action-adventure film playing in front of her eyes rather than real life.

She doubted she'd watch an action-filled movie ever again. Not that she'd seen very many. Give her a silly romantic comedy any day.

She tore her gaze away and tried not to dwell on the murder of a man she'd once dated.

"Eve? Did you already give the officer your statement?"

Startled from her thoughts, she turned to Grayson. "Yes. He spoke to me briefly while you were talking to Rhy and the others."

"Okay, great. Ready to get out of here?" He used the key fob to unlock the door. "Jump in. We'll get breakfast."

"Breakfast?" she echoed incredulously, not moving an inch. "You want to eat after seeing Andrew's dead body?"

He grimaced. "I know it sounds awful, but yeah, I'm hungry. Besides, we need to eat sometime. Better to do that now on the way back to the hotel."

She placed a hand to her stomach, warding off a queasy sensation. Maybe it was a cop thing, to be able to shrug off death so easily. She was secretly glad she hadn't had to see Andrew up close and personal. "I'll go with you, but I can't eat."

He hesitated, then nodded. "Okay, but I have a great place in mind, Rosie's Diner. You'll like it. She bakes fresh pastries every day."

With a sigh, she pushed off from the truck to get inside. Leaving the scene of the crime was a relief. She wished now she hadn't agreed to visit Andrew first thing in the morning.

Although if they hadn't found him, he may have lain on the floor for days. No, it was probably better that they'd come. Bad enough he'd probably been there all night.

Grayson cranked the air and pulled away from the curb. "Do you really think a woman did this?"

He was asking her? "I don't know. I only wanted to point out that it's possible. Could be that Bambi or the other women he dated had anger issues and didn't take kindly to being cheated on."

"We'll use the computer to see if we can find Bambi," he said as he headed east. "She shouldn't be too hard to find with a unique name like that."

"She may be listed in the O&P website too." It was easier to focus on Bambi than on how Andrew had died.

"The Brookland cops have called in a Detective Meyer

to handle Andrew's murder, so I can't reach out to Bambi myself." Grayson sounded as if he were talking to himself more so than to her. "But maybe we can find something by digging through her social media posts."

"Rhy is okay with giving Brookland control over Andrew's case?" She was surprised by that.

"For now. We really don't have anything concrete to link Andrew's murder to the attacks on you." He shrugged. "But if we do come up with something that connects them in even the smallest way, Rhy will yank the case back quicker than you can blink."

That sounded more like the Rhy she was getting to know. Funny how the entire team came across as family, not just friends. Maybe that came from depending on them to watch your back.

Grayson was an integral part of the team. Casting him a sidelong glance, she agreed with him on one thing, he was different now than he was in high school. Mature, focused, and intense on the task at hand. Willing to risk his life for her and the public. She had to admit he'd become a better person over the years.

Depressing to realize she had pretty much stayed the same. Not that her research wasn't important, but at the moment, it didn't seem nearly as noble.

"Wow, Rosie's is packed," he said, breaking into her thoughts.

"A sign of good food, right?" She glanced around the small parking lot. "I think there's someone leaving."

"I see them." He wrenched the wheel of the truck in time to scoot into the spot vacated by a minivan. "I think I smell cinnamon rolls."

"You're imaging that." When she pushed out of the

truck to head inside, she realized he was right. The scent of cinnamon hung in the air.

"I was right!" Grayson's dark eyes gleamed. "You'll want to try them, Eve. I've never tasted anything like it."

For some reason, her appetite seemed to have returned. Maybe Grayson had been right about getting back to a feeling of normalcy. On the surface, they looked like a couple out for a meal. Not finding dead bodies or hiding from bad guys.

There was one empty booth, and Grayson made a beeline for it.

"Ach, Grayson, it's good to see you, lad!" A large woman with bright red hair that had to have come from a bottle of dye greeted them warmly. "And who is this fine lass you've brought with you?"

"This is Dr. Eve Shaw," Grayson said.

"Just Eve is fine," she quickly interjected. "Grayson has told me so much about you."

"About me, or my baking?" Rosie arched a brow and laughed. "Ach, I'm teasing you, lass. Make yourself comfortable. I'll bring you coffee and cinnamon rolls."

"I love you, Rosie," Grayson declared. "Thanks so much."

Eve had to smile when Rosie blushed like a schoolgirl. Minutes later, they had steaming mugs of coffee and two of the largest cinnamon rolls she'd ever seen in her life.

"I can't eat all this," she protested. Then she took a bite and nearly moaned. "Although it's really good."

"I'll finish what you can't." Grayson had eaten part of his too. "I told you they were the best."

Her guilt over being alive while Andrew wasn't faded a bit. Andrew hadn't been big on attending church with her, even though he had claimed he believed in God. She hoped he was being truthful and that he was in a better place now.

"Hey." Grayson reached across the table and took her hand as if reading her thoughts. "If there is a link to Andrew's death and the attacker, we'll find it and bring the murderer to justice. We should pray for Andrew too."

"You're right. I completely forgot." She set down her cinnamon roll and bowed her head. "Dear Lord Jesus, we thank You for this food we are about to eat. We pray Andrew is up in heaven with You. We ask for Your guidance and strength as we seek those who hurt him and Pauline. Amen."

"Amen," Grayson said. "That was a nice prayer."

She was surprised he'd thought of it. She clung to his hand for a moment. "I hope you do find the person responsible. And soon."

"We will." He gently squeezed her fingers then reached for his coffee. Rosie returned to take their breakfast order.

Grayson ordered the full Irish; she settled for two eggs over easy and toast. Rosie was bringing their food a few minutes later, when she heard someone say, "Grayson? Is that you?"

"Hi, Alanna." He smiled at a beautiful blonde standing beside a tall, dark-haired man. "Hey, Reed. You have the day off?"

"Yes, we both do for once." Reed smiled at Alanna who looked up at him adoringly. She realized this was Alanna Finnegan now Carmichael, and her husband. "We plan to head to the lakefront later this afternoon."

"Sounds like fun. Oh, this is Dr. Eve Shaw. Eve, Alanna and Reed Carmichael. I mentioned Alanna is one of Rhy's sisters."

"Of course. It's nice to meet you."

"Do you work at Trinity Medical Center too?" Alanna asked. "I work as a nurse in the Emergency Department."

"No, I don't take care of patients. I have a PhD in molecular biology." Her tone was apologetic.

"A super smart woman, huh?" Reed teased. He socked Grayson on the shoulder. "She's way out of your league, bro."

"Trust me, I'm well aware. We went to high school together; she's the only reason I passed advanced chemistry." Grayson grinned. "I'm not sure I ever thanked you for your help, Eve."

"You don't need to thank me." She could feel her cheeks growing warm. Reed was teasing Grayson as if they were a couple when they weren't. And she had no idea how to set the record straight. "I would have helped anyone I was partnered with."

"Ouch, she zinged you good," Reed joked.

"Yeah, yeah," Grayson grumbled. Then he took a bite of the cinnamon roll. "Yum. See what you're missing?"

"You're killing me," Reed muttered. "I want one."

"Hey, a table just opened up." Alanna tugged on Reed's arm. "Let's grab it before it's gone."

"Later," Reed said, turning away.

Still embarrassed, she concentrated on eating her food. Thankfully, Grayson had taken the ribbing in stride. She quickly changed the subject. "Are we heading back to the hotel after this?"

"Yeah." Grayson licked his fingers after finishing the cinnamon roll. "Why? Did you want to make a stop along the way?"

"I wouldn't mind some toiletries and a change of clothes." She didn't want to sound ungrateful, but she'd felt like a frump next to Alanna.

"We'll pick something up at the discount store along the way. If that's okay with you."

"Thanks."

Rosie beamed with pride when they'd both polished off their meals. So much for not feeling hungry. They didn't linger over coffee, fully aware of patrons waiting in the doorway, so Grayson paid the bill, and they quickly left.

The stop at a local department store didn't take long. Soon they were back in the Timberland Falls Suites. She took her bag of toiletries and change of clothes into her room, shut the door, and headed to the shower.

Then she abruptly sat on the commode, the events of the morning welling inside. First Pauline died in the explosion, and now Andrew had been murdered in his home.

And she couldn't shake the feeling that the killing wasn't over.

Deep down, she knew it would not end until she was dead.

GRAYSON BOOTED up the computer while Eve showered and changed. He was determined to find everything he could about the infamous Bambi. He searched the Owens and Powers Pharmaceutical page but didn't find a list of reps listed there as he'd hoped. Undeterred, he went to social media.

To his surprise, there were several Bambis to pore over, and lots of them were pretty women.

Since he'd need Eve to pick out the correct Bambi, he went back to a basic search engine. There was a social media site that was for professionals, so he thought that might be the best place to find Bambi the pharmaceutical rep.

Bingo. He found Bambi within two minutes. She looked sweet and innocent in her professional photo, and he found himself staring at her and wondering if she had hated Andrew enough to take a hammer to the back of his head.

Glancing at his watch, he frowned upon noting the time. Eve had been in her room for almost thirty minutes. Was something wrong? He rose to his feet as his phone rang. Seeing Rhy's name on the screen, he picked it up.

"Did you find something?" he asked in lieu of a greeting.

"The Brookland Police have arranged for Bambi Altman to come in for questioning, but it sounds like she has a solid alibi for the time frame of the murder," Rhy informed him. "There was a department meeting yesterday that went well into the evening, and she and several other sales reps went out for drinks afterward. The Brookland PD will validate she was there, but it doesn't look like she's involved. Detective Meyer said she sounded very broken up and upset over learning of Thomas's death."

"She could be a good actress," Grayson pointed out, still looking at her photo on the screen. "But the alibi will likely clear her. Did the ME give any indication about time of death?"

"Roughly between eight and ten o'clock at night. He won't say more until he's finished the autopsy."

"Yeah, that makes sense." He'd imagined the guy had come into the kitchen to get water or something to eat, heard the doorbell, let the person in despite being dressed in just a pair of shorts, then was killed without warning. "What about a toolbox?"

"No sign of a toolbox," Rhy confirmed. "Meyer agrees with you that the killer brought the hammer with him."

It wasn't much to go on. Even less to connect this murder to the attacks on Eve. "I was hoping for more," Grayson said.

"They're working on it. I just thought you should know about Bambi's alibi." Grayson heard a voice in the background before Rhy continued. "I have to go. Keep Eve safe. My gut says she's in more danger than ever."

"I will. Stay in touch." Grayson disconnected from the call, battling a wave of frustration. It was hard to keep Eve safe when he didn't know anything about the motive behind the attacks against her.

Or where the next attempt would come from. Would it be another bomb, like the one planted in the Jeep? A gunman showing up like at the American Lodge?

Not a hammer, he felt sure of that. Even if the hammer wasn't part of Andrew's toolbox, the motive for bringing it to his condo was definitely premeditated murder.

"Yeah. That's Bambi."

He turned to find Eve coming up behind him, her gaze seemingly locked on the computer screen. "You can see why Andrew was taken with her."

"I don't think she's anything special." In his mind, Eve was the one who looked amazing. He liked it when she wore her long brown hair down, framing her face. "You look great."

She blushed. "I'm just glad I could take a shower. Did you find anything interesting on Bambi?"

He filled her in on the information Rhy had provided. "I don't think the interview with her will reveal anything new, but I'll check in with Detective Meyer later."

"She has an alibi, huh?" Eve looked disappointed. "I told you the hammer was strange, though."

"Yes, no toolbox in the house the way you suspected." He shrugged. "Don't take this the wrong way, but it seems to me that a woman likely used it on Andrew. A guy who was upset with him would have gotten more satisfaction out of beating him with his fists."

She smiled. "None taken, but if the intent was to kill Andrew, a hammer is more likely to get the job done."

"There is that." He gestured to the chair beside him. "Please sit down. I think we should start at the beginning. Maybe there's something we missed."

"I don't see what we could have missed." With a shrug, she sat beside him as requested. "But I'm willing to try."

"I keep coming back to this being related to your research in some way," he admitted. "How many people knew about your live presentation?"

She frowned. "I don't know. It wasn't a secret, but I didn't go around blabbing about it either."

"Did you discuss it at lunch with the other assistant professors?"

"No. I tend to eat lunch at my desk. We don't have a cafeteria in the research building. I'd have to walk over to the College of Medicine or to the hospital. That would be a waste of time, so I don't bother."

He thought her life at work and at home seemed lonely but didn't mention it. "It's possible your colleagues didn't know about it?"

"Well, it's posted on the website. If they bothered to look. I don't check it regularly, but if someone was curious enough, they could find information there."

"Website?" This was the first he was hearing about it. He pushed the computer toward her. "Show me."

Her slender fingers flew across the keys. She brought up the research institute's website and turned it toward him. "See? There are many presentations listed here."

He leaned forward and scrolled down the page. "The one you were going to give is still on here."

"It is? Hmm. Firestein said we'd reschedule. He must not have updated it." She tapped the screen. "But you can see he's listed there as the moderator. I was going to present a portion of my research, then field questions."

"Anyone could find this." The thought was depressing. Instead of moving the case forward, he felt as if they were sliding backward down a steep hill with nothing to stop them.

"If they knew where to look." She bit her lip. "I guess I should have mentioned this earlier. Sorry about that."

"It's okay. Not your fault. Things have been happening fast." And maybe that's what the killer was counting on. Frequent attacks to keep them off balance.

He rose to his feet and paced, trying to understand where they could go from here. The research. This had to be about her research.

Maybe he was making it too complicated. He spun on his heel to face her. "Your boss, Dr. Roger Cannon, knew about the presentation, but he wasn't at the research institute when the bomb went off."

"Right. So?"

"He lives in Brookland, and that's where Andrew's condo was located." The connection was so thin it was basically transparent, but it was all he could come up with. "We need to call him, set up a face-to-face meeting."

"Okay, I can do that," she agreed. "But I don't think he's involved."

"You've said that about all your colleagues, Eve. I know

you don't want to consider the possibility that someone close to you did this. But everyone is a suspect until they're proven innocent."

"I hear what you're saying. But my five-million-dollar research grant doesn't just pay for my research, it supports the lab too. Roger would be shooting himself in the foot by getting rid of me."

"Five million?" he repeated. "That's a lot of money."

"Not in the world of research," she said with a shrug. "The overhead is a lot, and there's my time, too, and the supplies. Like I said, my grant funding benefits the entire lab. And that includes the work Roger is doing."

"He is in a similar field as you are?" He was feeling more stupid by the minute.

"No, he's working on something else. But I'm just saying that he works out of the same lab. Uses the same instruments. If any of them are even left," she added grimly.

Was he going down the wrong path? Then again, from where he stood, there weren't any clear roads to follow. "Let's talk to him."

"Whatever you want is fine with me. But he may not pick up a call from a strange number." She dug the disposable phone from her oversized bag.

He listened as she made the call, explaining to Roger that her phone was lost and that she was using a friend's line to call him. She politely requested a call back and left the new number.

He was about to ask how long it would take for him to respond when her new phone rang. She answered. "Roger? It's Eve. Yes, I'm fine, although I am devastated to learn about Pauline."

There was a pause as she listened to whatever her boss

was saying. He wished he'd told her to put the call on speaker.

"Roger, I'm with a police officer who would like to talk to you. Can you spare some time today? Really? Great. Um, sure, we can meet at your home in Brookland. I remember where it is. I know, I feel bad the research institute will be out of commission for a while. Okay, we will see you in an hour." She lowered the phone. "Looks like we're heading back to Brookland."

"Okay, I'll get Rhy to assign backup." He wasn't about to approach a possible suspect alone. Not after the way they'd stumbled across Andrew Thomas's dead body. "I'm glad you gave us some time to work with."

"I can push the meeting back further if you'd like. It sounds like he's at home anyway since the research institute is off-limits." She frowned. "He said the insurance company won't let anyone come to work until they've inspected the building for safety."

"Yeah." He wasn't surprised by that. He called Rhy, but the call went to voice mail, so he tried Joe.

"You've been busy," Joe said.

"And I need more help. I was hoping you'd send some of our teammates to back me up at the home of Roger C. Cannon." He got straight to the point. "He's Eve's boss, and I don't like the idea of going there without support."

"Yeah, sure. I can spare Roscoe and Jina," Joe agreed. "What's the ETA?"

"We're meeting him in Brookland in an hour." He provided the address that Eve hastily scribbled on one of her infamous sticky notes. "It's probably overkill, but I wasn't expecting to find Thomas dead either."

"I agree with you taking extra precautions," Joe said. "What do you hope to learn from this guy?"

"I don't know," he said honestly. "It's a long shot, but I'm hoping he'll know if one of her colleagues was more upset over her promotion than she knows about."

"Okay, keep us in the loop," Joe said. "Roscoe and Jina will meet you there."

"They'll probably get there before we will, so have them scope the place out for me."

"Understood. Later." Joe ended the call.

He looked at Eve. "We'll leave soon."

"We'll be early, but it sounds like you want it that way." She rose and stuffed things back into her oversized bag. "I hope your teammates don't scare Roger and give him a heart attack."

"They won't. Trust me, Roger won't know they're nearby." He took a few minutes to use the items he'd purchased at the discount store. Returning to the main living area, he found Eve was ready and waiting, her bag slung over one slim shoulder.

He'd parked Zeke's truck along the side of the building, with the rear of the truck closest to the building so they could make a quick getaway if needed. And this area of the lot was out of view from the front lobby. Scanning the area, he kept Eve between him and the wall as they made their way to the truck. He held her door for her, then went around to the driver's side.

He'd barely gotten behind the wheel when the sharp crack of gunfire echoed around them.

"Down, get down!" He leaned over to push Eve's head below the dashboard while grabbing his own weapon. The fourth attempt was yet another gunshot, but now he didn't dare start the truck either, fearing there was a bomb hidden in the undercarriage.

The situation was spinning way out of control. And he had no idea how to stop it.

CHAPTER NINE

Eve's heart thundered in her chest as Grayson covered her body with his. She prayed that God would keep him safe from harm. She heard him calling 911, his voice incredibly calm in the face of the crisis.

"Shots fired outside the Timberland Falls Suites. Officer requesting assistance."

She squeezed her eyes shut, trying to quell her shaking. The only good news was that the gunfire had stopped. At least for the moment. Maybe because they were crouched so low in the truck that the shooter couldn't see them.

"Maybe we should drive out of here," she whispered.

"Negative. I don't know if he planted a bomb under the truck."

That hadn't occurred to her, although based on everything that had transpired, it should have. She braced herself, knowing that if the shooter had a trigger of some sort, he could set the bomb to blow at any moment.

Although if he had the ability to do that, why try to shoot them? None of this made any sense.

Grayson spoke again. "Joe, we're taking gunfire at Timberland Falls Suites. Please send Jina or Roscoe here ASAP. We're in Zeke's truck, but I don't dare start the engine."

She couldn't hear Joe's response, but she knew the team would rally around them. It was a comforting thought in the face of danger.

The team would always be there for Grayson and for her by proxy.

She had never experienced anything like it. God had sent Grayson and his entire team to her side when she needed him the most.

"Are you okay?" It took a minute for her to realize he was speaking to her.

"Peachy." She was far from okay and suspected he knew that. But what was the point of complaining? It wasn't his fault.

"I don't know how we were found here," Grayson murmured. "I feel like I let you down. I didn't notice anyone following us from Rosie's or Andrew's condo, but the shooter must have found a way to track us."

"You didn't let me down; we're alive because of you." She wanted to lift her head to look at him, but that was impossible. She was feeling slightly claustrophobic from the cramped position but told herself to get over it.

"The shooter is likely gone." He lifted his head, giving her slightly more room to shift. "Stay down, though. I'm going to slide out of the truck and look underneath."

"Why not wait for the cops to arrive?" She couldn't hide her panic. "The gunman may be waiting to get a better shot at you."

"I don't think so. He'll know I've called for backup. If

he's smart, he'll get out of Dodge. I'll use the truck as protection." Grayson sat up and pushed his driver's side door open so that he could get out.

She lifted her head just a few inches to watch him. True to his word, he stayed low, crouching alongside the truck. Then he went down on his hands and knees, examining the undercarriage.

It was a task he'd done several times before, but she couldn't get over how Grayson approached it as part of a normal routine. Nothing about searching for a bomb was normal.

The silence was broken by the wail of sirens. She was impressed by the quick response of the Timberland Falls police department. Maybe because they didn't often get reports of gunfire in the quiet suburb.

Grayson was probably right about the gunman being long gone. She lifted her head farther, easing the pressure on her stomach and chest from being bent in half. The sun was relentless. When she saw the twin bullet holes in the glass window, another wave of nausea hit hard.

So close. If Grayson hadn't reacted as quickly as he had, they would both be dead.

"Well, that figures," Grayson muttered.

Her stomach tightened. "You found a bomb?"

"No, I found a tracking device." He sounded upset with himself. "I should have thought of checking for one before leaving Andrew's condo."

"You think the same person who killed Andrew placed the tracking device on the truck?"

"Yeah." He came out from underneath the vehicle, his expression grim. "And that means the murder of your ex-boyfriend is definitely connected to these attacks."

She stared in horror. "If that's true, the killer must have been lurking nearby the entire time we were there."

"Yeah, or the killer came by early that morning to see if anyone had discovered the body yet and happened to see us pull up." He shook his head. "I'm surprised the perp didn't try to take us out then."

"Maybe he came along shortly after you called for back-up." She searched her memory, trying to envision those moments outside Andrew's house. "I didn't notice anyone driving past. Certainly no one walked by on foot."

"I should have done a more exhaustive search for the killer." He sounded annoyed with himself again. "It's not uncommon for murderers to return to the scene of the crime."

"Andrew had been dead a while, though, so why would you look for the killer?" She didn't want him to beat himself up over this. "It's not your fault, Grayson. You're doing your best to keep me safe."

"Too bad my best isn't good enough," he muttered.

"Don't—" she started to say, but she was cut off by the arrival of the Timberland Falls police department. Not one squad but three showed up, along with an ambulance.

"Come with me." Grayson held out his hand. She took it and allowed him to draw her from the truck. She resisted the urge to go farther until she'd reached in and snagged her bag. Maybe she had an unhealthy attachment to her research notes, but she'd carried them with her for this long, and she wasn't about to let them go now.

Grayson put his arm around her waist as they walked toward the three police cruisers. "Stick close to the cops, okay? This may take a while."

"I understand." No doubt they'd search for signs of the

shooter. She set her oversized bag on the ground, feeling weak and shaky. The adrenaline rush had faded, and all she wanted was to curl into a ball and cry.

Not an option. She willed herself to stay strong, listening as Grayson filled the responding officers in on the series of events. He then led them to Zeke's damaged truck, showing them the tracking device that had been placed beneath the rear bumper. She couldn't hear what they were saying, but the grim expressions on the officers' faces spoke volumes.

The policemen spread out to search. Grayson went with them, gesturing to a small, wooded area directly across from the Timberland Falls Suites parking lot.

Her chest tightened with fear as Grayson and the others cautiously approached the trees, their respective weapons drawn. The foliage was thick enough that the gunman could still be hiding in there.

Please, Lord Jesus, keep Grayson and the other officers safe in Your care!

She held her breath as they disappeared into the trees. When she heard a car engine, she jerked around in surprise. A black SUV pulled up behind the other squads, and she relaxed upon seeing Roscoe's familiar features.

"Eve? Are you hurt?"

"I'm fine." She gestured toward the woods. "Grayson and the other officers are searching over there."

"I'm sticking close." Roscoe took up a position beside her. "I know Grayson would want me to watch over you."

Stupid tears pricked her eyes. She blinked them away, staying focused on the trees across the lot. Thankfully, there were no sounds of gunfire, and soon a few of the Timberland Falls officers emerged from the woods.

"The shooter is gone." She couldn't decide if that was

good or bad. Probably bad unless they were able to find some sort of clue as to his identity. "I can't believe he tracked us here in the first place."

"How did he accomplish that?" Roscoe asked. His faint Texas twang was cute.

"Grayson said there was a tracker on the truck. Probably put there while we were outside Andrew's condo." Chilling to imagine the killer watching them discover Andrew's dead body. "Grayson is kicking himself for not checking for one."

Roscoe snorted. "He's being too hard on himself. I wouldn't have looked for one either. I think the way the danger keeps escalating is getting to him."

As if hearing their discussion, Grayson emerged from the woods. His expression was difficult to read, but she noticed he carried a small plastic envelope in one hand.

"He's found a shell casing," Roscoe said with satisfaction. He lifted his hand, drawing Grayson's attention. He quickened his pace to join them.

"This is from a thirty-eight." Grayson held the bag up to show Roscoe the brass. "I only found one, though. He must have picked up the other one as I know two shots were fired."

"I see the two bullet holes," Roscoe agreed.

Grayson nodded. "This one had rolled beneath some leaves, so he missed it. Maybe he left in a hurry because he knew the Timberland Falls PD was on the way. Let's go look at the truck. Maybe the slug is inside."

She trailed after the two men going back to Zeke's truck. Seeing the bullet holes again only reinforced how close they'd come to being hit.

"I need a penknife," Grayson said. "I think the slug is in the back seat."

"Here." Roscoe handed one over. "Be careful not to hit the slug itself."

"I won't." She watched in amazement as Grayson sawed with the knife in the cushion around the entry point of the bullet. Then he plucked at the stuffing until he was able to pull it free. It wasn't easy, but soon he held out his hand. "I need another evidence bag."

Roscoe handed one over. Grayson dropped the slug with the stuffing around it inside. "That's one. Let's see if I can find the other."

She was impressed he'd found anything at all. He and Roscoe scoured the inside of the truck. "It passed through the back," Grayson finally said.

"Yeah, I see the exit hole." Roscoe shook his head in amazement. "I'm glad we found one of them. That should be more than enough."

"Yeah. But we still need a weapon to match." Grayson crawled out of the back seat as several Timberland Falls police officers crossed over.

"Hey, that's our crime scene," one protested.

"This is a crime that started in our jurisdiction," Grayson said. "If you'd like, I'll have my captain call yours."

"You do that," the officer said with a scowl.

Grayson handed the evidence bags to Roscoe and made the call. A few minutes later, he was speaking to Rhy. "Boss, we have a bit of a situation here. Shooter found us in Timberland Falls. I have a slug and shell casing as evidence. Timberland Falls isn't happy about us taking it from the scene." He listened for a moment, then handed the phone over to the closest officer. "He wants to talk to you."

The conversation was short and sweet. When the Timberland Falls cop handed the phone back, he turned away without a word.

"Nice work," Roscoe said. "Maybe we'll get prints."

"I hope so." Grayson grinned. "Guess Rhy got his way, huh?"

"Was there ever a doubt?" Roscoe asked. "I wouldn't want to get on Rhy's bad side, no way no how."

She stepped closer to Grayson. "Why do they care who takes the evidence?"

"It's a jurisdiction thing. Technically, the crime happened in their backyard." Grayson shrugged. "They'll get over it."

Roscoe gestured to his vehicle. "Do you still want to meet with the professor?"

"Yes, but we'll need to give our statements first. Is Jina in Brookland?" Grayson asked.

"Yep. She's keeping an eye on the place," Roscoe agreed. "Although based on the gunfire here, it's not likely the perp is hanging around Brookland."

"Probably not." Grayson shifted to look at her. "As soon as we give our statements, we'll get out of here."

She nodded. "My statement will be short. I didn't see anything."

"Me either. Just a flash of movement before the gunfire rang out." Grayson shook his head in disgust. "I'm not sure how he missed us, other than maybe the glare of the sun threw him off."

"God was watching over us." She reached out to touch his arm. "We're very blessed."

"She's right," Roscoe agreed. "The big man upstairs gets the credit."

"Which one of you is Officer Clark?" A man wearing a suit and gold badge crossed over to them. She figured he was the detective assigned to the case.

"I am." Grayson turned to face him. "I have reason to

believe the shooter was targeting Dr. Eve Shaw. This is a case we've been working for the past thirty-six hours."

The detective's gaze narrowed. "You're MPD? And hogging all the evidence? Why are you even here? Why did you bring danger to my neck of the woods?"

Eve stepped forward. "He's been trying to keep me safe, that's why. What, you don't get any crime here? This is the first time ever?"

"Whoa there, little filly." Roscoe's tone held amusement. "He's not the bad guy here."

She spun away, struggling to control her temper. She wanted to kick something but managed to stifle the urge. Her luck, she'd break her toes.

Somehow, she calmed down enough to give her brief and likely unhelpful statement. Then she grabbed her oversized bag and stood by Roscoe's SUV.

Maybe it was irrational, but she wanted nothing more than to get far away from this place.

Not that she would feel safe anywhere else. Depressing to think that no matter where they went, it seemed as if the killer would find them.

GRAYSON SQUELCHED a flash of guilt over keeping the two evidence bags. He didn't necessarily blame Timberland Falls for being upset, but it wasn't like he'd drawn the shooter here on purpose. And he knew the lab in Milwaukee would put a rush on the prints.

He doubted they'd find any, but he could hope.

"What happened?" the detective asked.

Stifling a sigh, he started at the beginning, how the bomb had been set in Eve's office to go off during her presentation and then finding another device at her home. He glossed over the other attempts, finishing the story with their stay here at the Timberland Falls Suites.

When he took a breath, the detective sighed loudly. "I hate when you guys come out here like this. Can't you stay in your own city?"

He glanced at Eve, hoping she didn't go after the detective again. "Look, we're trying to get to the bottom of this mess. I thought coming here would keep us safe. I was wrong. Sue me."

"Yeah, yeah." The detective scowled. "Go on and get out of here. I'll follow up with your captain on the investigation. The least he can do is to keep us updated on your progress in arresting this guy."

"Works for me. Thanks." He turned away, grateful that was finished. Surprisingly, the detective didn't ask Eve any questions. He nodded at Roscoe. "Let's hit the road."

"About time," Roscoe agreed. Soon they were heading toward Roger Cannon's home in Brookland. He called Jina on the way.

"See anything noteworthy?" he asked.

"Negative. The streets are busy with kids biking and playing, which is a bit of a concern. I don't like kids being in the line of danger, but honestly, I've been in position for a solid fifteen minutes without seeing anything unusual."

"Okay, we'll be there soon," he assured her.

"You may want to give the professor a head's up. I've seen him looking out the window as if waiting for you to show." Humor tinged her tone. "He seems anxious to get this meeting over with."

"Will do." He turned to look at Eve in the back seat. "Let your boss know we had a minor delay but we're on our way. Don't tell him about the gunfire, though."

"Okay." She dug in her bag for her disposable phone and made the call. "Roger? We're on our way. Sorry for running late, but we'll see you soon."

"You had to leave a message?" he asked.

"Yes. I don't know if he remembered which phone number I called him from." She shrugged. "He'll listen to the recording."

"Yeah." He turned back to stare out the windshield. "As soon as this interview is over, let's get the shell casing and slug to the lab."

"Will do." Roscoe glanced at him. "I'm surprised he used a handgun from that range. A rifle would have been better."

"Maybe he doesn't have a rifle," Grayson said. "The shooter outside the American Lodge had a handgun too. I think this guy prefers bombs but will take whatever shot he can get." He paused, then added, "I'll have to tell Zeke about the damage to his truck."

"He'll be fine." Roscoe brushed that concern off. "As long as you and the doc are safe."

"And he knows I'll pay for the damage." He scrubbed his hands over his face, feeling as if he'd failed big time. "I never expected a shooter to show up at the hotel."

"Hey, we'll find him." Roscoe lightly punched him in the arm. "He's making mistakes now, leaving the shell casing and slug behind. And it's so hot he may not have bothered with gloves."

"Yeah." He hoped Roscoe was right. They needed a break in this case big time. And while he still wanted to speak with Roger Cannon, he wasn't sure the guy would be of much help.

They arrived at Brookland twenty minutes late for their original meeting time. Grayson hadn't seen any sign of Jina, but the team sharpshooter knew how to blend in and stay out of sight.

Roscoe dropped them off. "I'm going to drive around a bit. Jina is right about the kids swarming around; school must be out for the summer. Call me when you're ready to roll."

"Got it." He reached for Eve's hand. "Let's do this."

"I'm ready." She looked calm after her angry outburst earlier. He had to admit, it was cute the way she'd jumped to his defense. She didn't understand that cops were territorial and didn't appreciate crossover criminal activity. And he hadn't taken the cop's comments seriously. In the end, they got to retain the evidence, which was all that mattered.

They walked up to the front door that immediately opened, revealing a man in his fifties, with salt-and-pepper hair and hunched shoulders. "Eve, I'm glad to see you." The older man's gaze shifted to him. "And you must be Officer Clark. Please come in."

"Thanks. Call me Grayson." He held the door open for Eve, who went in first. The interior of the house was blessedly cool. He glanced around curiously. The interior was neat and rather formal, maybe picked out by the younger, pretty wife. Not nearly as lived in as the Finnegan homestead. "Thanks for meeting with us."

"Of course. Have a seat." Roger waved toward the living room furniture. "I would like an update on the investigation."

"I'm sorry, but there's not much I can tell you." Grayson sat beside Eve on the sofa. "We're still searching for the person responsible for the bombing. That's why we've come here."

"Why?" Roger Cannon's eyebrows shot up. "I don't know anything."

"Where were you when the bomb went off?" Grayson asked, undeterred by his response.

"Here at home." Roger frowned. "I was leaving my house when I received a call from the police letting me know the research institute was on fire. At first, I thought something went wrong in the lab. I had no idea a bomb had been set."

Roger sounded sincere enough. "Why were you running late?"

Roger flushed. "I overslept, but that was mostly because I'd stayed up late reading the latest *JAMA*. I'm usually an early riser."

"*JAMA*?" He glanced at Eve questioningly.

"*Journal of the American Medical Academy*," she clarified. "It's one of the top research journals."

"I see." That sounded plausible too. He decided to switch directions. "Which of the associate professors is holding a deep grudge against Eve?"

"What?" There was a flash of something that looked like guilt in the man's eyes. "None of them. We all work as a collaborative team."

"Cut the bull," Grayson said bluntly. "This isn't a TV interview, it's a criminal investigation. A female scientist gets promoted over a bunch of men who are not only older than she is but who have been working longer at their respective research, and you claim none of them are holding a grudge? Sorry, Professor, I'm not buying that."

Roger's gaze darted toward Eve, then back to him. "Okay, fine. There were a few rumblings when I gave Eve the promotion. What does it matter? I highly doubt any of them would set a bomb in the building."

"Not just the building, in her office." Grayson wanted to grab the professor by the shoulders and shake him. "Don't be obtuse. This is a personal attack against Eve, and you know it. Her office was bombed, and another device was placed at her home. She's been targeted nonstop over the past thirty-six hours. Now tell me which of her colleagues complained the most bitterly about her promotion."

"I don't know any such thing!" Roger blustered. Although the older man avoided Grayson's gaze. "This is the work of an extremist group, not someone within the institute. Destroying the lab hurts us all."

"Roger, please." Eve spoke up for the first time. "I need to know who resents me. It doesn't mean he's guilty of anything, but it's important we rule him out so we can move on to other suspects."

Roger abruptly threw up his hands. "Okay, you want to know the truth? All of them. Is that what you wanted to hear? Each one of the associate professors who were passed up came to see me personally to express their dissatisfaction with my decision."

Eve went pale as if she'd been slapped in the face. Grayson put his arm around her shoulders to help steady her. As bad as he felt for her, they were finally getting somewhere. "Any of them more upset than the others?"

Roger ran his hand through his salt-and-pepper hair. "Nick Strong. He called your research ridiculously overrated and threatened to go to the dean to file an age discrimination lawsuit against me. I told him to go ahead, that your work spoke for itself." Roger shrugged. "I knew your work was great, Eve. You don't get awarded five million dollars in grant money by offering substandard research. Nick was just upset, that's all. I'm sure he didn't mean it."

"Did he file the lawsuit?" Grayson asked.

"Not that I'm aware of," Roger admitted. "I assumed the

dean talked him out of it. It's not as if Nick is even close to the age of fifty. He wouldn't have a case."

So, Nick Strong, the guy known to have lost his temper once before had threatened to sue the research institute over Eve's promotion.

As far as he was concerned, the guy had just made it back up to the top of his suspect list.

CHAPTER TEN

They all resented her. Eve worked hard not to show her feelings, but she was deeply hurt to hear that every single one of her colleagues had gone to Roger to express their anger over her promotion.

Meanwhile, they'd all said nice things to her face. Told her how proud they were of her success. Smiled as they'd congratulated her. Exuberantly praised her innovative approach to research.

Lies. It was all a pack of lies, and she felt sick at the thought of that resentment possibly bubbling up like molten lava into murder.

No, despite Roger's description of Nick Strong and his ridiculous lawsuit, she still had trouble believing it. Or maybe she just didn't want to. She'd worked with these men every day for the past five years. *Years!*

She pressed a hand to her chest as if that would ease the pain in her heart.

"Is there anything else?" Roger asked, interrupting her train of thought. "I don't mean to sound ungrateful, but I have work to do."

"So do I." The words snapped out of her mouth before she could stop them. "But I'm not able to work since someone keeps trying to kill me."

Roger's expression was pained. "I know how hard this must be for you, Eve. And I'm sorry. But I'm sure the police will get to the bottom of this very soon."

She nodded, not trusting herself to speak. Being angry with Roger wouldn't help. She supposed it was good of him to stand by his decision in the face of adversity. It would have been easier for him to promote one of the others in that good old boys' network that still existed in the upper echelon of the world of academia.

"I need the addresses and phone numbers for each of Eve's colleagues," Grayson said. "Then we'll leave you to it."

"Oh, well, I don't know," Roger hedged. "I don't think I'm supposed to give out personal information."

"That's fine. I'll get a subpoena." Grayson thumbed the screen of his phone. "Joe? I need a subpoena . . ."

"Never mind, I'll give you the information." Roger capitulated with a shrug. "If Eve had access to her computer, she'd be able to find it as well."

"Joe, I'll call you back." Grayson ended the connection as Roger turned to his office.

A few minutes later, Roger handed Joe a sheet of paper. "I know you have to look at everyone, but I honestly don't think anyone who works at the research institute would do something this drastic."

"Clearing them is the best way to prove that, isn't it?" Eve said, wondering when she'd started sounding like a cop. "Thanks for being honest with me."

"I'm sorry," Roger said.

"Me too." She turned away, suddenly anxious to get out of there.

Grayson caught her hand, giving it a reassuring squeeze. She managed a smile as Roger walked them to the door. It seemed overkill now to know that Jina was out there somewhere watching the place.

"Roscoe? We're ready," Grayson said into his phone.

Less than a minute later, Roscoe's SUV came around the corner to pull up in front of Roger's home. Grayson held the back passenger door open for her so she could climb in. Then he jumped up front.

"I'll let Jina know she's off duty." Grayson texted her via his phone. "I have a list of names and addresses of possible suspects. We just learned these men were upset over Eve's promotion. We'll need to vet them all, but I'm most interested in Associate Professor Nick Strong."

"What's his address?" Roscoe asked. "We can head there now. But you'll want to let Jina know to head over too."

"You're right. No more surprises." Grayson's thumbs flew over his phone screen.

Her stomach clenched as Grayson rattled off the information after texting Jina. She wasn't sure she was ready to face Nick. Or any of her colleagues for that matter. But she didn't protest.

Would Nick be surprised to see them? Would he admit to threatening a lawsuit over her promotion or pretend Roger was exaggerating?

And why did her heart ache so badly over hearing how much her male colleagues resented her? She'd known going into this line of work that being a female researcher in a male-dominated profession wouldn't be easy. She wasn't the first woman to succeed in a way that threatened men.

Or the last.

Still, it hurt. Mostly because she honestly hadn't known. In a way, she wished she still didn't.

"Strong's house is only two miles from yours, Eve." Grayson twisted in his seat to face her. "Did you know that?"

"No. We don't have that sort of relationship." She knew now she didn't have any semblance of a relationship with Nick or the others. "I've never been to his place, and to my knowledge, he's never been to mine."

Grayson held her gaze for a moment, then nodded. "Okay. Hopefully, he'll be home so we can talk."

"Yes, I'm sure he'll be there." At least that's what she'd be doing, working in her home office if going to the institute was unavailable.

Unless, of course, Nick was out somewhere trying to track her so he could kill her.

No. She pushed that negative thought out of her mind. There was no sense in thinking like that. Not without proof.

Yet she couldn't seem to shake the feeling of impending doom.

The trip didn't take long. She noticed Roscoe drove slowly past the house first without stopping. It was a blue and white ranch home, bigger than she'd have expected. She reminded herself that Nick was roughly five years her senior, although he wasn't married as far as she knew.

Divorced? She may have heard something about that. To her shame, she hadn't paid much attention to the personal lives of her colleagues. They always discussed research since no one else really understood their world the way they did.

Now she could admit that may have been a mistake. In more ways than one. Not only was she open about her research, but she hadn't bothered to get to know her colleagues outside of the lab.

"Park a few blocks away," Grayson directed.

"You'all planning to sneak up on the place in broad daylight?" Roscoe drawled.

"No, I just want to give Jina time to get into position." Grayson's tone sounded defensive. "And yeah, okay, maybe I don't want to broadcast our presence just yet."

"I hope Roger didn't call ahead to warn him," she said with a sigh. "Although it's not like you're going to arrest him."

"Not yet," Grayson said. "But if we can find something to link him to the bombing, I will gladly slap cuffs on him."

She had no doubt about that. It would be easier all the way around if Nick was the guilty one. Grayson and Roscoe could throw him in jail, and she could move on with her life. Her boring, myopic life.

For some reason, digging back to her research didn't hold the same appeal as it had prior to all of this. Her eyes had been opened to the outside world, and it suddenly hit her that her life would never be the same.

Because she wasn't the same person she was prior to the explosion in her office.

She lifted her gaze to the blue sky outside her passenger window. This was all a part of God's plan. She only hoped she'd have the strength and courage to move forward in the way God expected of her.

GRAYSON COULDN'T HELP glancing frequently at Eve. He knew she was still struggling with the information her boss had shared about her colleagues. Roscoe must have noticed because the Texas transplant arched a brow.

Ignoring his teammate, he stared down at his phone, waiting to hear back. It was a long couple of minutes before his phone vibrated with an incoming text.

"Okay, Jina is in place. She's in a car parked on the next block over with a view of the front door between two residences." He glanced up at Roscoe. "You're right about the fact that we can't sneak up in broad daylight. I'd like Eve to stay here while I go up and talk to him."

"No, I'm coming too," Eve said, interrupting him. "He's my colleague."

He suppressed a sigh. "I don't think he's going to admit anything if you're standing next to me." He turned to look at her. "Please, Eve, I'm asking you to trust me on this."

She didn't like it but slowly nodded. "Fine. I'll stay put."

"Thank you." He was relieved he didn't have to force the issue. "Keep her safe, Roscoe. Give me a few minutes to walk over."

"Will do." Roscoe gave a curt nod.

Grayson slid out of the SUV before Eve could say anything more. He walked up the street and then went around the block, sweeping his gaze over the area. He had to assume Nick Strong was armed and dangerous.

It was always better to be safe than sorry.

As he approached the blue and white ranch-style house, he didn't see any movement from inside. He strode up to the front door and knocked.

No answer.

Feeling a sense of déjà vu—this was exactly how things had started at Andrew Thomas's condo—he knocked again. Then leaned on the doorbell. He could hear the chimes of the bell pealing inside.

Still no answer.

He gave it a full five minutes before pulling out his phone. He had programmed all the contact numbers of Eve's colleagues into his phone. He called Nick Strong's number, hoping the guy would answer.

But he didn't. After three rings, the call went to voice mail. He pondered that for a moment, imagining the guy ignoring a call from an unknown number.

He sent a text identifying himself as Officer Grayson Clark requesting a moment of his time.

There was still no response.

Glancing around, he wondered how many of Strong's neighbors were watching him. He didn't see anyone peering out their windows, but he had to assume there was at least one nosy Nellie out there. He moved to the closest window and looked inside. At least this time he didn't see anything resembling a dead body.

He next moved to the garage, going around the corner to take a quick look into that window too. There was no vehicle inside.

Having found nothing suspicious to warrant a forced entry, he turned away. Talk about a massive letdown. He'd hoped to interview Strong sooner rather than later.

Lifting his phone, he called Roscoe. "I got nothing. No vehicle in the garage, no response at the door. He hasn't taken my call or responded to my text."

"We'll be there in a few," Roscoe assured him.

He lowered the phone, texted Jina with the disappointing results that she could no doubt see for herself from her position, then waited for Roscoe. When the black SUV pulled up, he quickly slid inside.

"I think it may help if I call him," Eve said. "He might respond to me, alone."

"No way." He turned to scowl at her. "He needs to know the police are involved."

"He already knows that since you texted and called, right?" She held his gaze. "He may respond better to me."

"I agree, let her make the call," Roscoe said. "It makes sense that he would prefer talking to her over a cop."

He wrestled with a flash of anger. Roscoe could at least pretend to be on his side. "You can call him but do not even think about setting up a meeting alone with the guy."

She shrugged and pulled out her disposable phone. Then she asked, "What's the number?"

He gave it to her. She made the call, and again, Nick Strong didn't pick up. "Nick, it's Eve. I'm worried about you after that explosion in the research institute. I'm wondering if we're all in danger and was hoping I could talk to you. Please call me back at this number, thank you." She sighed. "I guess we'll see if he calls me back."

Maybe it would work if Strong did call her. She could set up a meeting, but Grayson would be the one to face the guy rather than Eve.

"Now what?" Roscoe asked. "You want to go down that list?"

He hesitated, considering their options. "Yes. Maybe the word will get out that these interviews are no big deal."

"Next address," Roscoe said, glancing at him expectantly.

They went to Geoff Abbott's house. This time, he didn't bother to send Jina ahead of time, telling her to head back to the precinct instead to update Joe and Rhy.

As it turned out, Geoff Abbott wasn't home either, which he found suspicious. He turned in his seat to face Eve. "Do your colleagues spend a lot of time together outside of work? Maybe have a favorite hangout?"

"I don't know." Eve stared down at her hands. "I know that sounds awful of me, but I honestly don't know much about their lives outside of the lab."

He found that strange; he and the rest of the team knew a lot about each other. Maybe except for Roscoe, who was the newest member of the team, having just joined them in January to replace Kyle, their murdered teammate.

"I think Allan is married," Eve abruptly said. "Or at least he has a photo on his desk of him with a pretty woman about his same age."

"Allan Ballard?" He double-checked his list and remembered how Ballard was one of the guys in the elevator when the bomb went off. "Okay, you don't happen to have the wife's name, do you?"

"No." She stared down at her hands again. "I feel like a failure. I don't know much about any of their personal lives."

"Hey, you're not a failure." He reached back to rest his hand on her knee. "You're brilliantly focused. You said it yourself, people's lives will be changed because of your research. Don't minimize that."

"I'll try not to." She didn't look reassured.

"Maybe if you take your time, a few more details will come back to you. And if not," he hastily added, "it's okay. That's what interviews are for, to gather information. Sooner or later we're bound to find one of these guys at home."

"It's no wonder they didn't like me." She sighed, then covered his hand with hers. "I appreciate your kind words. All I can do now is to move forward, right?"

"Exactly." He smiled.

She released his hand and tucked her hair behind her

ear. "I'll keep trying to come up with details I may have deep in my subconscious."

"That's my girl," he said, turning back to glance out the window. "Are we close yet to Ballard's house?"

"No, that one happens to be in White Gull Bay," Roscoe said. "Probably not too far from Steele and Harper's place."

"Okay. Can't hurt to check it out." Even though logically he knew any of these coworkers could be responsible, he kept going back to Nick Strong and his anger management issues. Well, to be honest, it was only one anger management documented with an arrest more than fifteen years ago, but from what he could tell from Roger Cannon's body language, the guy had not held back while loudly voicing his opinion of Eve's promotion. And her, what had he called it? Oh yeah, ridiculously overrated research.

To his surprise, Allan Ballard answered the door when he knocked. Eve had agreed to wait with Roscoe again, although he wasn't sure that allowing Roscoe time alone with Eve was smart on a personal level. Oddly, he didn't like the idea of Roscoe flirting with her.

"Dr. Ballard? I'm MPD police officer Grayson Clark. Do you have a minute to talk about the bomb at the research institute?"

Ballard looked just like what Grayson would imagine a frumpy professor would. He wore a baggy T-shirt paired with flannel pants and bedroom slippers. The guy was likely only in his early forties, but his pale skin and thinning hair and thick glasses made him look older.

"I already gave the police and the arson investigator my statement." Ballard did not invite him in. "I have nothing more to add."

"Did you resent Eve Shaw enough blow up her office and her research notes?"

His blunt question rocked the guy back on his heels. "What? Of course not. That's a horrible thing to say."

"You know that bomb was meant for her, though, right?" Grayson pressed.

Allan's eyes widened. "No, I had no idea. Everyone has assumed this was the work of one of those nut job groups."

"Everyone? Who exactly have you spoken to?"

Now Allan shifted his weight from one foot to the other. "We've all discussed this terrible event. Those first few hours after it happened, I was getting one call after another."

"Okay, if that's the case, why didn't any of you call Eve?" Grayson wasn't buying his story. Oh, he didn't doubt they'd all been talking, but he felt certain they'd all known Eve was the target. Hence the reason they hadn't reached out to her.

"Who are you again?" Allan demanded, narrowing his gaze. "Why aren't you in uniform?"

"I'm working undercover." He flashed his badge. "I would like to know why none of Eve's colleagues reached out to her after the bombing."

There was a long moment before Allan grudgingly replied, "Roger said he'd spoken to her and that she was okay. We didn't want to bother her. Now if you'll excuse me, I need to get back to work." Allan stepped back to close the door.

He could have forced his way in but chose not to. For one thing, he could not imagine this guy carrying a weapon and shooting at them. Sure, he might be smart enough to make a bomb, but setting it, lying in wait, and then pulling the trigger? That was a stretch.

Dejected, he headed back down the sidewalk to the road. He waved at Roscoe who was parked just a few car lengths down the street.

"You really need to let me talk to my coworkers," Eve said the moment he'd gotten seated.

"Maybe." He couldn't deny he hadn't gotten much out of Allan Ballard. "Three down, two more to go."

"We haven't met with Nick Strong or Geoff Abbott yet," Roscoe pointed out.

"I know, but we can try to take care of the last two. I could be wrong, but I don't see Allan Ballard as a threat."

"I could have told you that," Eve said in exasperation. "Allan won't even walk up a few flights of stairs. He claims he has bad knees, but I think he's just out of shape. He eats a lot of junk food, and his idea of exercise is walking into work from the parking lot."

He realized he should have asked her opinion ahead of time. "Okay, I hear you. And I agree with your assessment."

"Of all my colleagues, he's probably the one with the most legitimate complaint," she went on. "His research is related to tracing DNA-related cancer genes and could be viewed as more important than what I'm doing."

"You're not giving yourself enough credit," he protested. "Your boss promoted you because of the quality of your work, Eve. That's the most important thing to remember."

"That and my five-million-dollar grant," she said with a sigh.

Yeah, he couldn't exactly argue thepoint. No matter what field of work a person pursued, money talked.

As Roscoe was about to pull away, another car came down the street from the opposite direction. He tensed and reached for his buddy's arm. "Incoming."

"I see it." The sun shone brightly off the windshield, so

he couldn't get a good view of the driver. But in moments, the car drove past and pulled into a nearby driveway.

"False alarm," he said with a rueful smile. "Let's head to the next house." He consulted his notes. "Larry Kimmel."

"He's more physically fit than Allan, but not by a lot," Eve said. "I think he's divorced, but I can't honestly say for sure. Could be that Geoff is the one who is divorced."

"Of all the men you work with, are any of them particularly close friends?"

She frowned. "I don't know. They've never indicated to me that they're friendly outside the lab. But Geoff and Nick are the closest in age. And out of the five associate professors, they're probably the most agile—going to the gym, keeping in shape, that kind of thing."

He made a mental note to check out the local pubs near the research institute. It would not surprise him to learn that Nick Strong and Geoff Abbott attended the same gym and hung out for drinks after work. Especially if they were two single guys.

What he truly did not understand was why neither of the single guys had asked Eve out. She was smart and beautiful, but maybe they didn't want to date a colleague. Or maybe they just didn't like women.

No one was home at Larry Kimmel's home either. His enthusiasm over having the names and addresses began to wane. The last name on the list, Jason Lamont, was home with his wife and a screaming toddler in the throes of a meltdown. The guy's eyes were red-rimmed and bleary with lack of sleep.

"Any word on when we can get back to work?" Jason had asked, a hopeful note in his voice. It was clear the guy was anxious to get away from his wife and child.

"No, I'm afraid not." He almost felt sorry for Lamont,

knowing Steele and Harper had similar bad nights with their daughter, Amelia. "How much do you resent Eve for her promotion?"

"Huh?" Jason blinked, then flushed. "Oh, you must have spoken to Roger. Look, I like Eve, but I have a family to feed." He gestured behind him. "The extra money would have come in handy, you know?"

"Yeah. Thanks for your time." He turned away, mentally crossing both Jason and Allan off the list of suspects. Two down, but far too many to go.

He rubbed the back of his neck as he jogged back to where Roscoe and Eve waited. "I don't think Jason is our guy; he's got a wife and toddler."

"He does?" Eve's voice reeked of surprise. "How could I have missed that?"

"Maybe he doesn't talk about his family at work." He wasn't sure what to say, how to make her feel better about learning this information about her colleagues. He couldn't see Jason following Eve with a gun, leaving his wife home alone with the baby.

"I never saw a family photo in his office," she muttered to herself. "I would have said something like, hey, nice family."

"Try not to stress." His gaze narrowed on the dark-gray SUV driving toward them. The same color and model as the vehicle he'd noticed outside Ballard's home.

"Hit it!" he ordered Roscoe just as the vehicle slowed. "Eve, get down!"

The words barely left his mouth when her passenger window shattered beneath the force of gunfire. Roscoe hit the gas hard, sending them lurching away from the scene.

Yet Grayson knew one well-placed slug in their gas tank

would prevent them from getting very far. He pulled his weapon, lowered his window, and fired back at the gunman, hoping to hold them off just long enough for Roscoe to make their escape.

CHAPTER ELEVEN

For what seemed like the zillionth time, Eve had her head tucked between her knees as gunfire echoed around her. Grayson was firing back at the vehicle behind them while Roscoe was calling for backup. She braced herself for the worst, especially the way Roscoe was taking sharp turns at a high rate of speed. The jerky movements kept throwing her off balance, but she did her best to stay seated with her head out of the line of fire.

Obviously, the man shooting at them wasn't Jason Lamont or Allan Ballard; there wouldn't have been time for either of them to jump into a car and follow them. Then who? She couldn't imagine Bambi doing such a thing.

One of the professors who wasn't at home? Was it possible Grayson was right about Geoff or Nick being involved?

"Good job, Roscoe, you lost them," Grayson said. "Thanks."

"Did you happen to get a look at the shooter?" Roscoe asked. "A description would be helpful."

"No. There was no front plate on the SUV, and the sun

glare off the windshield made it impossible to get a good look at the driver. Eve? Are you okay?"

She lifted her head to look at Grayson. "I'm fine, but how did the gunman find us? I don't understand why this keeps happening."

"I don't know." Grayson's dark eyes were intense. "You have blood on your cheek. A piece of glass must have cut you."

She lifted her fingers and felt the damp blood. "It doesn't hurt."

Grayson shook his head. "I'm sorry. I don't know how we were found, but I have a theory. One you won't like hearing."

"Roger called the professors to warn them we were coming to talk to them," she guessed. "And that means either Geoff, Nick, or Larry could be responsible."

"Yes." He held her gaze before turning away. "I need to talk with Rhy and Joe about issuing a BOLO for the three of them."

"A BOLO? How can you arrest them when you can't prove they've done anything wrong?"

"BOLO stands for *be on the lookout* as a person of interest," Grayson clarified. "And we can bring them down to the precinct for questioning. That's different from arresting them."

She swallowed hard and turned to gaze out her broken window. Maybe it would be for the best if the police brought her colleagues to the station. She couldn't take much more of this. Her research was suffering, and at the rate things were going, it would take months just to get caught up.

"What's going on?" a deep male voice asked through the

car speaker. She glanced up to see Rhy's name on the screen.

"Roscoe's SUV has suffered gunshot damage, but everyone is fine," Grayson said.

"Where are you?" Rhy demanded.

Grayson explained about their plan to speak to Eve's associate professors. "Three of them weren't home, then a shooter shows up just after we leave the home of the last guy on the list, which is a hard coincidence to swallow. I'd like BOLOs issued for Nick Strong, Geoff Abbott, and Larry Kimmel as persons of interest in the bombing of the research institute and attempted murder of Eve Shaw."

"Got it," Rhy said. "Any other description of the SUV the shooter was driving?"

"Dark gunmetal gray, no front license plate, and looked to be a new model, but that's all I can give you. Oh, and there is likely a bullet hole in the windshield too."

There was a brief, heavy silence as Rhy digested that. "Okay, I can put the word out to glass repair companies to alert us if they are called to fix a bullet hole in a windshield, but that will take time. It's possible the repairs could be done prior to us reaching out."

"Have Gabe double-check that none of the professors owns a gunmetal-gray SUV," Grayson continued. "I'm sure they're smart enough not to use their own vehicle, but there's always a chance they borrowed something from a family member or close friend."

"Good idea. I'll get Cassidy and Flynn involved as well. You know, I think it's time for you to take Eve to the safe house in Ravenswood."

Eve frowned, wondering what he meant. Did the police really have a safe house where they kept citizens who happened to be in harm's way? That seemed impractical on so many levels. She couldn't be the first woman to be in a situation like this.

"Yeah, you're probably right," Grayson agreed. "But I think we need a clean vehicle first since it's possible the perp in the gunmetal-gray SUV got our license plate number."

"Go to the car rental in Brookland," Rhy said. "I know the manager and can arrange for a replacement."

"Two vehicles, boss," Roscoe piped up. "Once Grayson and Eve are safe in Ravenswood, you'll need me in the field. These visits to the professors have heated things up. We may need to stake out their homes."

"Good point," Rhy agreed. "Grayson, let me know when you get to the safe house."

"Will do."

She watched as Roscoe ended the call. "Is the safe house a place I can work on my research?"

"I can't let you log into work," Grayson said with a frown. "But going through your notes should be fine."

"Okay." His response wasn't a surprise, but she'd thought it wouldn't hurt to ask. "I wonder if we should talk to Bambi too."

"Yeah. I doubt she's the one shooting at you, but she may have some insight into this," Grayson said.

"Don't let Raelyn, Jina, or Cassidy hear you talk like that," Roscoe chided. "Our three teammates are very good with firearms, especially Jina."

"That's true," Grayson agreed. "Yet there's a big difference between a pharmaceutical sales rep and cops."

"For all we know, Bambi's dad was a cop and taught her everything he knows." Roscoe flashed a grin. "Most of the gals in Texas shoot as well or better than the men."

"That's only because Texas is the wild, Wild West," Grayson shot back.

Roscoe barked out a laugh. "Yep, you'all are right about that."

Eve tried not to be annoyed by their banter, understanding they were trying to ease the tension. They were accustomed to being in danger, but she wasn't. Yet she also didn't want to complain in case they decided to leave her behind.

She still felt that she would have gotten further with her colleagues if she'd been able to speak with them directly. Even if hearing the truth about how much they resented her hurt.

"You okay, Eve?" She glanced up to see Roscoe looking at her with concern in the rearview mirror.

"Fine." She forced a smile. "I'm getting used to the sound of gunfire."

Grayson twisted in his seat to look at her. "I'm sorry. I know I promised to protect you, and things haven't gone as planned. Trust me, you'll be safe at the house in Ravenswood. The home has been constructed with bullet-resistant glass."

"Oh, great." Was this what her life had come to? Being taken and held in a safe house with bulletproof glass?

She struggled not to break down crying. Grayson had asked her to trust him, and she did. But she had trusted her boss and her colleagues, too, only to find out she barely knew them. Hadn't known about Jason's wife and baby, hadn't known how much they'd resented her. How Nick had threatened to file a lawsuit.

How well did she really know Grayson? Sharing an advanced chemistry class in high school ten years ago didn't mean anything.

She had never felt so acutely alone as she did right now.

———

GRAYSON COULD TELL Eve was hanging on by a thread, and it was all his fault. He shouldn't have taken her along to talk to her boss and her colleagues. It didn't matter if he wanted to work the case, he knew the smart thing would be to get Eve into the Ravenswood safe house and keep her there until they had the bomber/shooter in custody.

Roscoe pulled into the rental car company that was located within a mile of the Finnegan homestead. And a short distance to Andrew Thomas's condo.

He needed to reach out to the Brookland PD detective about his interview with Bambi Altman. It was possible Detective Meyer would talk to him since he knew Rhy and the rest of the Finnegan family.

If not, he'd try reaching out to Bambi himself. He didn't want to interfere with the Brookland investigation, but if Meyer had already spoken to her, there was no reason he couldn't talk to her too.

The two rental SUVs were waiting for them, so all Grayson and Roscoe had to do was to sign the paperwork, grab the key fobs, and go.

"I'll follow you to Ravenswood," Roscoe offered. "Make sure you get there safely."

He hesitated. "You can go ahead. I'm going to stop at the Brookland PD first. See if Detective Meyer will give me an update on Andrew's murder."

Roscoe frowned, glancing at Eve. "I can do that for you."

"I'm sure we'll be safe enough at the Brookland PD."

The minute the protest left his mouth, he winced. What was he doing? Hadn't he just told himself to let the team handle the interviews. "Never mind," he hastily amended, "I'll call him."

Roscoe sighed. "We'll go to Brookland PD together. You know as well as I do Meyer will just dodge your calls."

He grinned in relief. "Thanks, Roscoe. It's a short detour, then we'll head to Ravenswood."

Eve didn't say anything, seeming to stare off into space. He kept a wary eye on her as he drove to the police department. She was probably still reeling from learning the truth about her coworkers resenting her, followed closely by yet another attack of gunfire.

He was doing a lousy job of protecting her. Was this how Steele, Brock, and Raelyn had felt over the past few months? They'd been in similar situations, which had thankfully turned out okay.

So why did he feel like a big fat failure?

Roscoe stayed right behind him during the short drive. Grayson pulled into the parking lot and waited for Roscoe to park beside him before getting out of the vehicle.

Eve pushed out of the driver's side, coming to stand beside him. "This won't take long," he told her.

"It's fine." Her tone was listless.

He wanted to pull her into his arms, but Roscoe had joined them, so they headed inside. The blast of air-conditioning felt good, but he noticed Eve shivered.

Slipping his arm around her waist, he urged her forward. "I'm MPD Officer Grayson Clark. I'd like to speak to Detective Meyer."

The front desk officer frowned. "He's busy."

"I know. I'm the one who called in the homicide. I only need a few minutes, and we're happy to wait."

"I'll let him know, but he may not have time to meet." The desk clerk picked up the phone and spoke in a low tone.

Grayson turned away, giving Roscoe a shrug. "Let's hang out for a few minutes."

"Okay." Roscoe nodded.

The minutes ticked by slowly. When ten minutes had passed, he wondered if they were wasting their time. Maybe Meyer had no intention of coming out to talk to him.

A door opened, and a stunning blonde stepped out, followed by Detective Meyer. The familiar face clicked in his brain.

Well, well, if it isn't the infamous Bambi Altman.

"Thank you, Detective," she said in a syrupy voice. "I appreciate everything you're doing to find Andy's killer."

"Take care," Meyer said in a noncommittal tone that led Grayson to believe the seasoned detective wasn't necessarily buying the grieving girlfriend act. "I'll let you know if I have more questions."

"Of course." Bambi gazed up at him. "Anything you need. I want Andy's murderer caught and punished for what he did."

Meyer's caught Grayson's gaze and gave a slight nod, indicating he'd be over to talk to him soon. Bambi left the police station without giving him, Roscoe, or Eve a second look. And honestly, he found that odd. Most people were curious enough to glance at strangers. It was almost as if Bambi wanted nothing more than to get as far away from the cops as soon as she could.

No one said a word until the door closed behind Bambi and she walked out of sight. Then Meyer gave him a resigned nod. "I can pretty much tell you she gave us nothing. Her alibi checked out. No one would want to hurt

Andy, he wasn't cheating, she wasn't cheating, and everything between them was hunky dory."

Grayson nodded thoughtfully. "What's your gut telling you?"

Meyer spread his hands. "I think their relationship was more than just personal, even though she denied that. I have no proof, though; we're still going through Thomas's phone records. And that will take time since he received dozens of calls from other nurses and providers."

"Yeah, that figures." Grayson wasn't sure why he'd thought the detective would be further along with the investigation. They'd only stumbled across Andrew Thomas's body, what, five hours ago?

"I can confirm they had a personal and professional relationship," Eve said. "I saw them together at work and at Andrew's condo. And I also have to tell you he always preferred being called Andrew, not Andy."

Meyer nodded. "I hear you. I tried to pin Bambi down on the last time she saw him, but she claims it's been a few days and was not able to be more specific."

Grayson and Roscoe exchanged a glance. "Okay, anything else that you can tell us? We're still trying to understand if Andrew's murder is connected to the violent attacks against Dr. Shaw."

"Nothing yet, autopsy won't be until tomorrow, and the drug screen takes time." Meyer scowled. "If you do find a connection between the two cases, I hope you'll let me know."

"Of course. Thanks for the update." He was glad Meyer had been decent enough to fill them in, so he added, "We have issued a BOLO for three of Dr. Shaw's colleagues. It's possible one of them may be responsible for the attacks against her, although I have no idea why any of them would want Andrew Thomas dead."

"That's interesting," Meyer said. "I'll make sure our guys keep their eyes open for them too."

He nodded and turned to Eve. "Ready to go?"

"Yes." Her faint smile didn't reach her stormy gray eyes. Once they were outside, she said, "I'm glad Meyer wasn't fooled by Bambi's act."

"Most cops are smart enough to look through that type of thing," he assured her. "Beauty is only skin deep, Eve. Doesn't matter how she looks on the outside if her heart is ugly."

"I don't know for sure that she's an awful person," Eve said. "Other than she wasn't above using her looks to make a sale."

He thought about that for a moment as they got settled in the rental SUV. He wondered how much sway a physician's assistant could even have when it came to prescribing medications. Granted, Andrew may have switched his patients over to whatever drug Bambi was pushing, but he was one man in a huge medical facility.

In the big scheme of things, his influence had to be a drop in the bucket. So why had someone killed him?

Much like the attacks against Eve, it didn't make any sense.

Swallowing his frustration, he backed out of the parking space and headed toward Ravenswood. The city was roughly twenty-five miles from here. He glanced at Eve. "Are you hungry? I'm not sure there's any food at the safe house."

"It does seem as if breakfast at Rosie's was a long time ago." She glanced over her shoulder to look out the back window. "Does Roscoe want to stop for food too?"

"I'll call him." He and Roscoe had taken a few minutes to pair their phones with the SUV's communication system prior to leaving the rental agency. He told the computer to call Roscoe, and ten seconds later, his buddy answered.

"What's up?"

"We're stopping for lunch if you're hungry," he said.

"Sounds good. I'll follow you."

"Thanks." He ended the call. "Anywhere in particular you'd like to eat?"

"Anyplace is fine." She still seemed out of sorts. "A salad would be nice."

He remembered a family restaurant that was about halfway to the safe house. They had just about everything under the sun on their menu. Not the delicious baked goods like Rosie's but plenty of other options.

Traffic was light on this warm summer day. It was too bad they couldn't head to a park or down to the lakefront for a picnic.

"Tell me about pharmaceutical sales reps." He glanced at her as he navigated traffic. "Do they have full run of the hospital?"

"Not at all," she said quickly. "Andrew was breaking the rules letting Bambi in. There are strict no sales rep policies because the hospital administration doesn't want patients exposed to expensive drugs when those generic or well-established medicines are often just as effective."

"So how did Andrew manage to break the rules?"

"I don't know." She frowned. "I supposed it's easy enough to blend in by wearing a lab coat and pretending to be a staff member."

It still wasn't enough to justify murder. "Did Andrew mention that Bambi was meeting with other providers? Doctors or physician assistants?"

She arched a brow. "You mean other *male* doctors or PAs? I doubt women would buy into her act."

She had a point. "Okay, other male providers, then."

"No, he didn't say." Eve looked away. "It's not like we had an extensive conversation about his cheating."

"No, I guess not." The more he thought about it, the less likely it seemed that Andrew's murder was connected to the attacks against Eve. Other than the suspicious timing, it was hard to imagine how they were tied together. For all they knew, Bambi had another jealous boyfriend out there somewhere who decided to eliminate the competition.

They drove in silence for a while, each lost in their own thoughts. He pulled into the restaurant, relieved that the hour was late enough that they had missed the noon lunch rush.

Again, he waited for Roscoe to pull up alongside them. With Eve between them, they headed inside.

"Booth?" the hostess asked.

Grayson glanced at Eve who nodded. "Thanks, that works."

Once they were seated, Eve next to him and Roscoe across the table from them, a harried server brought waters and menus.

"I'm starving." Roscoe scanned the menu. "Ooh, barbecued ribs!"

They often joked that when Roscoe retired from the police department, he would open his own barbecue restaurant. He always ordered barbecued ribs or chicken, then complained that nothing was as good as a Texas barbecue.

When their server returned, Eve ordered her salad, while he chose the steak sandwich. He and Eve stuck with water, and Roscoe ordered a coke.

"Do we need to pick up groceries before heading to the

safe house?" Eve asked. "I'm not a great cook, but I can make something simple like spaghetti."

"We'll have groceries delivered," he assured her. "And I love spaghetti."

"Not as good as ribs," Roscoe declared.

Eve wrinkled her nose. "I'm not a fan of ribs."

Roscoe comically placed a hand over his heart. "Stabbed by the pretty doc," he complained.

Eve reluctantly smiled, and he was glad she seemed to be getting over their recent setback. She was beautiful, not in a flashy way like Bambi—who he wouldn't trust as far as he could throw her—but in a wholesome girl-next-door kind of way.

He pulled himself from those inappropriate thoughts. He needed to remember how badly things ended with Monica. "I'll need something to work on while we're holed up in the safe house. If Gabe hasn't gotten around to checking our three perps to see if they own gunmetal-gray SUVs, maybe I can dig into that. I wish we had enough to get a warrant for rental car agencies to give us information."

"We don't, not without narrowing the search parameters," Roscoe pointed out. "Maybe if you saw a rental car decal or sticker, that would be enough."

"I didn't." Sometimes he got tired of the bureaucratic red tape, yet without the proper search warrants, their evidence could easily get tossed when it came to going to trial. "Hopefully, the BOLOs will yield results and those interviews will produce enough evidence for a judge to consider granting a warrant."

"Anything is possible," Roscoe agreed.

Their food arrived. Eve bowed her head to pray. Beneath the table, Grayson reached for her hand.

"Dear Lord Jesus, we thank You for this food and for keeping us all safe in Your care. Amen."

"Amen," he murmured.

"Amen," Roscoe echoed. Then he grinned. "Dig in!"

Shaking his head at Roscoe's antics, he took a bite of his sandwich. It was good. He and Roscoe made quick work of their meals while Eve picked at her salad.

A phone rang, making him and Roscoe check their pockets. To their surprise, Eve pulled out the small disposable phone.

"Who could be calling me?" she asked. Before he could advise her not to answer, she lifted it to her ear. "Hello?"

Had to be a wrong number or spam, he thought.

"Oh, hello, Dave."

Dave who?

"Oh, um, I hadn't thought about when it would be a good time to reschedule my presentation," she said, giving him a clue. The name clicked; he remembered her talking to a Dr. Dave Firestein shortly after her office exploded.

He leaned forward to ask in a hushed tone, "How did he get your number?"

She waved him off. "Sure, a week from today should be plenty of time. Okay, thanks." When he scowled, she belatedly asked, "How did you get this number?" After listening for a moment, she said, "Okay, thanks. Talk soon." She ended the call.

"Let me guess, your boss gave him your new cell number," Grayson said. He should have considered that earlier.

"Yes. It's not a big deal; you didn't tell Roger not to share it."

"No, I didn't." But maybe he should have. He took another bite of his steak sandwich and wondered why this

Dave Firestein was so anxious to set up another live presentation. Then he reached for Eve's hand. "Where does Firestein work? Madison?"

"Yes, why?" Eve nibbled on a piece of grilled chicken.

He met Roscoe's gaze and was reassured that his buddy was thinking along the same lines as he was.

Madison was only an hour from Milwaukee. Close enough that Dave Firestein could have been the one to set the bombs, then head off to sit somewhere safe with a laptop with the presentation up on the screen, waiting for the blast.

CHAPTER TWELVE

Reading Grayson's expression, Eve shook her head. "Dave isn't involved. Why would he be?"

"It all comes down to your research, remember?" he pointed out.

"Just because Dave is a molecular biologist, too, doesn't mean he's in competition with me," she protested. "And even if he was, I cannot see Dave setting bombs and detonating them."

"You haven't wanted to believe it was anyone close to you," Grayson said softly. "And I understand that. It's not easy to look at people you've been working with for years as the enemy. But you need to keep your mind open to all possibilities."

It was hard to argue with that, but she still couldn't see it. Then she remembered how Roger had told her all her colleagues had been upset at her promotion. Every. Single. One.

She stared down at her half-eaten salad, feeling sick. How would she face them once this nightmare was over? Return to business as usual, acting as if she didn't know?

Nope. She was not doing that. It would be best to clear the air, confront them one by one about their feelings. She wouldn't apologize for being promoted, but maybe she could do better in being a friend. Maybe join them in after-work activities. If she was welcome.

"O'Dell's Pub." She didn't realize she'd said the words out loud until Grayson turned to stare at her. She flushed. "I'm sorry, I just remembered that Nick once mentioned O'Dell's Pub. It's not far from Trinity Medical Center. I believe many of the hospital staff go there after work."

"You're just remember this now?" Grayson asked with a frown.

"I know, I'm sorry." She felt like an idiot. "You asked earlier if the guys went somewhere after work, and I said I didn't know. But I think Nick mentioned O'Dell's. I never paid much attention to what they were talking about unless it involved research."

"It's okay." Roscoe offered a reassuring smile. "At least we know now when we can still do something about it."

"We should swing by the place," Grayson said. "Just to see if there's a gunmetal-gray SUV with a bullet hole sitting in the parking lot."

"I highly doubt either of these guys would be that careless," Roscoe said. "But it's worth a drive by."

"I'll call Melrose," Grayson said. "We'll get license plate numbers of Strong's and Abbott's personal vehicles from him."

"Don't forget Larry Kimmel," she added. "If we're going to check, may as well do all three."

"Good idea." Grayson shot her a smile, and she was relieved he wasn't upset with her. Why did her brain work like this? It was one of the reasons she had sticky notes everywhere. A thought would pop into her mind long after she'd read some article. Sometimes days later. Almost as if her brain had a longer than normal processing time.

It was both a curse and a blessing.

A blessing because even with the delayed response, she had been able to do great things with her research. But in this situation, it would have been nice to have remembered about O'Dell's sooner.

She took another bite of her salad, listening as Grayson copied license plate numbers down on a napkin.

"Thanks, Gabe. Appreciate the intel. Oh, one more thing. Will you please run the license plate registration for a Dave Firestein in Madison? I need the make and model of that one too." There was a brief pause as Grayson waited. He munched a fry as he waited. "Great. Thanks." He slipped his phone back into his pocket. "Unfortunately, none of our suspects drives a gunmetal-gray SUV."

"We always figured it would be rental." Roscoe looked thoughtful. "You know, I think that may be one way to get the information on the rentals. Call each company to see if anyone returned a vehicle with a bullet hole. We wouldn't need a warrant for that."

"I like it," Grayson agreed. "I'm sure they'd be willing to give us that information, especially as it's indicative of a crime. I can work on that when we reach the safe house, after we do the drive-by of O'Dell's Pub."

"I can do the drive-by," Roscoe offered. He used his phone to take a picture of the napkin Grayson had scribbled on, "while you and Eve head to the safe house."

Eve sipped her water watching Grayson. The way he hesitated told her he wanted to be there. Clearly, sitting on the sidelines while others worked the investigation wasn't in his DNA.

"We'll go together. It shouldn't take long," Grayson said.

He didn't look at her. "We won't be in harm's way. If we spot one of the vehicles, we'll call Rhy and have him send a couple of squads pursuant to the BOLO."

"Okay." Roscoe shrugged. "Suit yourself."

They finished their meal, the guys eating with a sense of urgency. She wished she'd remembered O'Dell's Pub earlier. Grayson paid their server with cash, leaving a nice tip, then rose.

"I'd like a bathroom break," she said in a low voice.

"Not a problem." Grayson turned toward the restrooms. "We'll all take advantage of the facilities."

Ten minutes later, they were outside climbing into the two rental SUVs. The temperature inside was stuffy, so she opened her window. Grayson did the same. His expression was somewhat grim as he backed out of the parking lot. O'Dell's was in the opposite direction of Ravenswood, and she could tell he was wrestling with his decision to go with Roscoe.

To be honest, she wasn't upset by the delay in getting to the safe house. Being alone with Grayson wouldn't be easy. She kept remembering their brief yet sizzling kiss.

One he'd shown no interest in repeating, much to her disappointment.

She settled back in her seat, scanning the scenery. Why hadn't she spent time enjoying the warm summer days? Her research was important, but she was keenly aware of the saying that all work and no play makes Johnny a dull boy. Or in her case, Jane a dull girl.

She was dull. Boring. One-dimensional in that she was always thinking of her research.

No wonder Andrew had found someone else. *Bambi,* she thought with a snort. He could have done better.

Now he was dead. Murdered in his own home.

Doing her best to push the depressing thoughts aside, she focused on the upcoming drive-by. Maybe this would work out. They'd find one or more of the cars in the parking lot, call Rhy's team to bring them to the station. Under pressure, they'd confess to their misdeeds, and the danger would be over. She'd head home and pick up her dull and boring life.

She silently promised to make changes, to broaden her horizons so to speak. Maybe take a short vacation. Something she'd never done.

And how pathetic was that?

"Roscoe? There are two parking lots. I'll take the one to the north of the building. You take the one across the street."

"Got it," Roscoe replied.

She was surprised at how busy the parking lot was during the daytime. Didn't these people work? Or maybe they were taking an extended lunch hour. She sat patiently as Grayson scoured the parking lot for one of four vehicles.

"I found one!" Grayson's excited tone had her searching for the vehicle in question. A white SUV with a license plate that started with AWO. He keyed the phone. "Roscoe? I have the vehicle owned by Geoff Abbott."

"Okay, sit tight. I'm still searching."

Grayson circled the parking lot and pulled into an empty spot at the end of the row. From this angle, she could just barely see the back end of Geoff's SUV.

The minutes dragged by slowly. Then Roscoe called. "I don't have anything over here."

"Okay, I'll call Rhy. Could be that Abbott and Strong drove together." As he reached up to disconnect the call, the brake lights of the SUV flashed.

"Did you see that?" Grayson asked. "I didn't see anyone inside, did you?"

"No." As she spoke, the white SUV backed out of the parking spot. She wondered if Geoff had managed to get into the vehicle while Grayson was circling the parking lot to find a place to park. "He's leaving!"

"I see that." He immediately put the gear shift in reverse and backed out too. Then he called Roscoe. "Abbott is leaving; I'm following him now. Call Rhy and then fall into place behind us."

As he spoke, Grayson shifted into drive and slowly followed Geoff's white SUV. She craned her neck to see if there was more than one person inside.

"I think he's alone," she said to Grayson, who was concentrating on following the car without being too obvious. He kept a decent amount of space between their two vehicles. At first she was worried they'd lose him, but then she noticed Roscoe's rental SUV coming out of the parking lot across the street.

Between the two of them, she felt certain they could stay on him. Yet as Geoff drove off, she couldn't help wondering if he was the one who'd bombed her office and taken shots at her.

Hopefully, they would have those answers and more once the other officers took him to the precinct for questioning. She believed in God's grace. Believed He was watching over them.

She silently prayed that God would guide them, keep them safe, and bring an end to the danger very soon.

GRAYSON WAS KICKING himself for not realizing Abbott had gotten in the car. Either the guy had been in there all along and he'd missed him, or he'd sneaked into the vehicle while he was circling the parking lot.

Either way, the near miss was unacceptable. He needed to stop being distracted by Eve and keep his mind on task. Before he managed to get one or both of them killed.

And where was Abbott's buddy, Nick Strong? For the past couple of hours, he'd wondered if the two of them had worked together in the plan to get rid of Eve Shaw. It would explain a lot, especially how they seemed to keep finding them.

The white SUV abruptly turned and headed onto the interstate, which was the opposite direction from where he lived. He keyed Roscoe's number on the screen. "Do you see this? Where is he going?"

"I'm not sure, but we can't lose him. Rhy's sending Flynn and Cassidy," Roscoe explained. "They'll be joining us soon."

"Tell them no lights and sirens," Grayson said. "I don't want to spook him. He could be heading to a meeting with Strong, Kimmel, or even Firestein."

"Roger that. I'll let them know," Roscoe agreed.

"If he goes all the way to Madison, we'll know he's meeting with Firestein." He glanced at Eve, who hadn't said much in the past few minutes.

"I thought of that possibility too." Her voice was quiet, as if she had finally accepted that one or more of her colleagues were likely responsible for these relentless attacks. "I guess we'll know soon enough."

"Yeah." He didn't like knowing he was putting her in harm's way yet again. Back at the restaurant, he'd known the right thing to do was to take Eve to the safe house, leaving the pub for Roscoe to deal with. Yet if he had done that, they may have missed Abbott's leaving.

He found himself silently praying that God would help him protect Eve. He needed all the support he could get.

Please, Lord Jesus, don't let me fail her!

Keeping track of the white SUV wasn't that difficult. It seemed as if Abbott was oblivious to his SUV being one car behind him, which would be unusual if the guy was responsible for committing these crimes.

Then the white SUV abruptly exited the interstate. Had Abbott finally noticed him? He took the same exit ramp, relieved to note that Roscoe was still behind him. The light was green, so he followed Abbott by turning right.

He called Roscoe. "Where are Flynn and Cassidy?"

"I just informed them of the turn," Roscoe said. "They're only five minutes behind us and closing fast. You did say no lights and sirens, remember?"

"Yeah, I know." He still thought that was for the best. "Thanks. Hey, he's turning into the parking lot of another restaurant."

"I see that. I think that place has a boat dock. Maybe he's meeting someone out on the lake?"

Since they were in the city of Peabody, he knew that was possible. Lake Michigan was the state's main attraction, but there were several smaller lakes, like Peabody Lake that boasted plenty of summer fun. "We'll lose him if he gets on a boat."

"Maybe we can rent one," Roscoe said.

Grayson knew that was a long shot but didn't argue. He pulled into the same restaurant parking lot, surprised at how big it was. Without hesitation, he parked in the first available spot, even though it was far away from the front of the restaurant that overlooked Peabody Lake.

"Hurry," he said to Eve as he pushed his door open. "We can't lose him."

She nodded and quickly hopped out of the car. He caught her hand, then broke into a light jog to get closer to the restaurant. There were plenty of cars, and he ground his teeth together in frustration when he noticed there were at least six white SUVs.

Where was Abbott? Battling a wave of panic, he raked his gaze over the area. There! He caught a glimpse of a man walking toward the restaurant. He hadn't gotten a glimpse of the guy's clothing while he was following from behind, but now he made a mental note of the dark-blue T-shirt and tan cargo shorts. He found it interesting that despite having a doctorate degree, Abbott dressed like any other thirty-something.

"That's Geoff," Eve said, confirming his thought. "Although he looks a bit down, as if he isn't looking forward to the meeting inside."

He nodded, having noticed the man's hunched shoulders and lowered gaze. Then he caught a glimpse of a phone. Abbott could be texting someone or maybe reading an email message.

His pulse jumped as he realized his instinct about Abbott working with Strong might be right on. And if so, he believed Strong was the one pulling the strings, dragging Abbott along with him. At first glance, Abbott wasn't giving off an aura of strength and determination. In his humble opinion, the guy appeared to be a follower.

He didn't have his police radio but hoped Roscoe would see them. He didn't slow his pace, wanting to get to the restaurant to get an ID on Abbott's cohort. The one obviously calling the shots.

Then Abbott abruptly turned away from the restaurant's main entrance to walk down a sidewalk that he assumed led to the lakefront.

"Do you think he's getting on a boat?" he asked in a hushed whisper.

Eve shrugged. "I don't know. There could be tables out front, too, right?"

"True." He wasn't sure what to expect and quickened his pace to catch up. They were jogging again, and he could hear the ragged breaths coming from Eve. He felt bad about pushing her physically but didn't dare slow their pace.

They were too close to lose Abbott now. At the very least he needed to get a glimpse of Abbott's partner.

When they reached the front of the restaurant, he slowed. There was no sign of Abbott with his dark-blue shirt and tan cargo shorts. The front of the restaurant was about halfway full of patrons enjoying the summer day. There were also over a dozen boats tied up at the pier with many more than that out on the lake.

Imagining the picture on Abbott's professional photograph on the website, he scanned the faces of those seated at the tables. Maybe Abbott had joined his partner at one of the tables.

Yet there was no sign of him. Not that it was easy to get a good visual of those sitting down.

"Grayson? He's on the pier," Eve said breathlessly.

He was? Narrowing his gaze, he scanned the pier, then saw him. Geoff Abbott awkwardly jumped into the back of a speed boat. Within seconds, a man who happened to already be on the boat released the ropes and pushed the vessel away from the pier. Abbott's buddy wore a baseball cap pulled low on his brow, masking his features. From here, he couldn't make out if there was a logo on the front.

Then the man in the baseball hat fired up the engine.

No! They were getting away!

He considered announcing himself as a cop and ordering them to stop, then decided against it. For one thing, they were far enough away that attempting to shoot was an empty threat. They could easily speed away without worrying about repercussions.

Besides, he didn't think Abbott or the man on the boat knew they were there.

As he battled with himself about what to do, Roscoe came up beside them. "Is that our guy?"

"Yeah." He shook his head. "I guess we can sit here and wait for them to return."

"Nah, let's find a boat and follow," Roscoe said with a grin. "I haven't driven a boat in a while. It will be fun."

"How can we get one? I don't see a rental sign," he protested.

"Money always talks," Roscoe said with a shrug. His gaze brightened. "Follow me. I see a good prospect now."

He followed his buddy down to the dock where a speedboat was approaching the pier. Roscoe flashed his badge, accompanied with a charming smile, and drawled, "Ma'am, would you mind helping a police officer?"

"Police?" the woman exclaimed. She was young, maybe in her thirties, and eyed Roscoe and Grayson curiously. "What in the world is going on?"

"I'll make it worth your while." Roscoe pulled out a roll of bills. "We'll only borrow the boat for a short while. I promise to have it back undamaged by the time you finish lunch."

"Ah, okay." The woman appeared flustered, and Roscoe offered a hand to help her off the vessel. Then he handed her several hundred-dollar bills and plucked the keys from her hand.

Seconds later, the three of them were cruising across Peabody Lake, searching for the red-and-white speedboat Abbott had jumped into.

"Call Flynn and Cassidy," Roscoe shouted above the sound of the engine. "Let them know we're on the water."

He made the call, barely able to hear Flynn's voice. Between their boat engine and others, along with the sounds of screaming from kids being dragged around in inner tubes, the noise was deafening.

"We're on the water, following Abbott and his accomplice," he shouted into the phone, hoping Flynn could hear him. "Stay at the restaurant. We'll keep you updated."

He thought he heard Flynn agree before he ended the call. Glancing at Eve, he found her huddled in the seat, hanging on to the side of the boat with wide eyes. It occurred to him this might be her first time on a boat.

"You okay?" he asked, lowering his head to speak in her ear.

She nodded, but the way she gripped the boat made him think otherwise. A quick glance beneath the front of the boat hull revealed a couple of life jackets. He grabbed one and held it out for her.

She released her grip long enough to put one arm through the opening and then the other. He zipped up the front of the jacket, tightening the straps so that it fit snug against her.

"Thank you." She tried to smile, but it looked more like a grimace. "I'm not a strong swimmer."

Yeah, he'd kinda figured that one out for himself. "We'll be fine. Don't worry. Roscoe seems to know how to handle a boat."

Again, she gave a curt nod, still holding on to the edge of the fiberglass vessel for dear life.

"Grayson, is that it?" Roscoe asked.

He went over to stand beside his buddy. Recognizing the white-and-red speedboat, he nodded. "Yep. You got it."

"I only see one person on board," Roscoe said.

They were far enough back that it wasn't easy to see details. He stared for long seconds, then caught a glimpse of a dark head. "Abbott is on board. He's slouched low in the seat next to the captain."

"I see him now." Roscoe kicked the speed up a few notches, but the other boat was also cutting across the lake as if in a hurry. Had they been made? Was it possible the two men were meeting a third? Firestein or Kimmel would be his guess.

Just how many of Eve's coworkers were involved in this?

"Don't let them get away," he warned.

"I'm on it." Roscoe grinned as if he were enjoying this. Normally, Grayson would have a similar attitude, but not when they had Eve on board with them.

And not when he was the one who'd placed her in danger. Again.

"I think they're slowing down," Roscoe called out. "Can you tell which house they might be approaching?"

He searched the shoreline for signs of someone standing outside waiting for Abbott and the guy in the baseball cap but saw nothing.

Then abruptly, the driver of the white-and-red boat abruptly hit the gas and swerved away from the shore, heading straight toward the middle of the lake.

What in the world? "Catch up to him," he shouted.

Roscoe didn't answer, handing the wheel as he did his best to follow their target. Grayson knew they must have been made, there was no other reason for the baseball cap guy to abruptly change course.

Minutes ticked by as Roscoe closed the gap between the boats. Grayson kept his attention focused on the white-and-red boat, praying they didn't lose them. Peabody Lake wasn't huge like Lake Michigan, but there were so many homes that he worried the other vessel would be able to hide in one of the numerous boat houses.

The ball-cap guy took another abrupt turn, a huge spray of water arching up as he switched directions. Roscoe tried to do the same, but another speedboat was coming toward them, pulling a young kid on an inner tube.

"Roscoe, look out!"

His buddy saw the boat and the kid and cranked on the wheel, going in the opposite direction from the course the red-and-white boat had taken. But Roscoe cut it a little too close, and he heard a squeal seconds before Eve lost her grip on the edge of the boat and tumbled into the water.

"Eve! Roscoe, kill the engine!" Grayson shouted. He lost his balance as Roscoe drew back the throttle. He tossed down his phone, kicked off his shoes and jumped up on the seat. There was no sign of Eve, but she had to be close by. Thankfully, he'd put her in a life vest.

There! Her dark head bobbed in the waves, her expression full of panic. Without hesitation, he dove into the water to go after her.

CHAPTER THIRTEEN

The water was surprisingly cold. Even with the life jacket on, she'd gone well below the surface before the vest buoyed her up to the surface. Eve gasped and choked, flailing her arms in an attempt to swim. Waves splashed water into her mouth, making her gag.

She wouldn't die here. The life jacket would keep her head above water. But the waves that kept splashing her in the face were difficult to handle. Every time she got a mouth full of water she coughed and nearly sank below the surface again.

Instinctively, she knew she had to calm down. Panic was making things worse.

"Eve!" Grayson was swimming toward her with strong swimming strokes. For the first time in her life, she thought it might be time to join a gym. Never had she felt more like a weakling than in these past few days. "You're okay. Just tip your head back and look up at the sky."

She did so, wondering why she hadn't thought of that herself. The waves still splashed into her face, but she didn't swallow nearly as much water this way. Finally, she stopped fighting and let herself drift in the water.

Then Grayson's arms came around her, lifting her up and out of the water. "You're safe now. I've got you."

She nodded, unable to speak, grateful for his reassuring presence.

"Roscoe! Over here!" Grayson held her with one arm, using the other to wave at Roscoe in the boat. She felt like an idiot that she'd fallen out of the stupid thing. She hadn't been prepared for the way the boat listed to one side during the sharp turns.

One minute she was hanging on to the edge, the next she'd been catapulted into the water.

She clung to Grayson as Roscoe brought the boat over. Roscoe didn't get too close but threw out a line for Grayson to grab onto. Grayson caught the rope and allowed Roscoe to tow them in.

Grayson lifted her up so that Roscoe could slide his hands beneath her armpits, pulling her up and into the boat. She slumped in the seat, her stomach rolling with nausea from swallowing so much lake water.

Moments later, as Grayson was climbing into the boat, she threw up.

"Sorry, I'm sorry." She battled tears. "I didn't mean to mess up the boat."

"Hey, it's fine." Grayson found a towel and sopped up the mess. "Don't worry about anything. The important thing is that you're safe."

"I lost sight of the red-and-white boat," Roscoe said with a sigh. He pushed the throttle forward, picking up speed. "I called Flynn and Cassidy, let them know we lost Abbott. They're going to drive around the lake to see if they can spot anything suspicious. We can continue to search for them on the water too. I'm sure the driver of the boat has pulled up to one of the piers."

"We could, but that will take time. The lake is over 2,400 acres, the likelihood of finding them is slim to none," Grayson said. "I think we're better off heading back to shore. It seems logical the ball-cap driver was taking Abbott to meet someone who owns property here. We'll ask Gabe to run a search."

Not only had she done the amateur move of falling out of the boat, but she'd also caused them to lose their quarry. She wished more than anything she could have done better, but there was no point in dwelling on her failures.

Lifting a hand to her drenched hair, she winced as she pulled a string of seaweed from the wet strands. She shivered as the wind struck her soaking-wet clothes as Roscoe sped toward shore.

"The place they were heading toward could be a rental," Roscoe pointed out. The two men were still discussing their options. Time for her to focus on what was important rather than her physical discomfort.

"Maybe, but based on how huge these mansions are, I'm going with an owner. Not a rental," Grayson said. She watched as he took his phone from a cupholder and thumbed the screen. Then he set it back down, as his clothes were as soaked as hers. "People who own these homes don't need rental income."

"You could be right about that, and it's a place to start," Roscoe agreed. He slowed the boat as they approached the restaurant. It was easy to pick out the well-dressed women who were seated at a table frankly watching their approach. Eve reminded herself that looks didn't matter, as she stood, water running in rivers from her soaked clothing. Grayson's clothes were just as wet, which made her feel worse that he'd had to rescue her. Although he still looked handsome, while she resembled a drowned rat.

"Take my hand." Grayson smiled reassuringly.

She allowed him to help her out of the boat and onto the pier. Then she unzipped her life vest and shrugged it off. He took a moment to store it on the boat, then grabbed his phone from a cupholder before jumping back onto the pier.

Avoiding the curious gazes, she tried to wring water from her shirt and capri pants. Her efforts were useless. She had one change of clothes in her suitcase, but that was back in the Timberland Falls hotel.

"Come with me," Grayson said, urging her away from the restaurant. She noticed Roscoe had gone over to the table to speak to the boat owners. "Roscoe will handle the boat issues. We'll head to the closest store to get us each a change of clothes."

"Thank you." She was glad he'd offered. "I feel bad for how things turned out."

"Don't," Grayson said with a frown. "I'm the one who should apologize to you. I shouldn't have brought you out here in the first place."

"It was important to follow Geoff," she said with a shrug. "I still can't believe he was on that boat. If you'd have asked me if Geoff had ever been out on a speedboat cruising Peabody Lake, I'd have laughed."

"I didn't get the impression he went willingly," Grayson said.

She thought about the brief glances she'd gotten of her colleague on the boat. Maybe Grayson was right about that. "Geoff is a nice guy. I can't imagine he'd willingly go along with some plan to sabotage my research."

"It's more than that," Grayson pointed out. "They've

been trying to kill you, Eve. Destroying your research is just an added bonus."

"Yeah." She still had trouble believing it. "We can try calling Geoff, see if he'll answer."

"He won't if he's in the middle of a meeting with the guy in charge." Grayson shook his head. "Besides, the boat fiasco has let them know we're getting close. Best thing we can do is find out who owns property on the lake."

She shivered, her shoes making squishing sounds as she walked. When they reached the rental SUV, Grayson opened the passenger door for her. "We're going to get the interior all wet."

"Yep." Grayson didn't look concerned. "Good thing it's a rental, huh?"

For the first time since she'd gotten on the boat, she smiled. She slid into the seat, wishing they had towels to soak up the water.

Grayson dropped his phone in the center console, likely to keep it dry. It rang as he was pulling out of the parking lot. Seeing Roscoe's name on the screen, he quickly answered. "How did it go with the boat owner?"

"They're fine," Roscoe drawled. "I made it clear they helped us with our investigation and thanked them profusely. I also paid them extra for the mess. Where are you heading?"

"The closest discount store." Grayson smiled at her. "We need to change, remember?"

"I can meet you there," Roscoe offered.

"No need. It's better if we can dig into the property owners on Peabody Lake," Grayson said. "Not to mention we still need to call rental agencies to see if any vehicles were returned with bullet-hole damage. Those are two items that are on the top of the list as far as getting another clue as to who is behind this."

"Understood. I'll check in at the safe house with you later. Meanwhile, I'll fill Rhy in on the Geoff Abbott angle and see if he has any other ideas."

"Thanks." He glanced at her questioningly. "Anything to add, Eve?"

"No, but thanks for everything, Roscoe."

Grayson ended the call, then gestured to the right side of the interstate. "There's a discount store over there, does that work?"

"Yes, I'm not picky." She glanced down at herself. "We're going to look silly walking through the store in wet clothes."

"That's okay. It won't take too long." He took the exit and drove straight to the store.

She did her best to ignore the curious stares as they grabbed a cart and hit the clothing section, then the shoe department. She added a few toiletries too. As did Grayson.

The entire shopping expedition took longer than she'd expected since they had to replace everything they wore including their undergarments, plus other essentials. Grayson also swung through the grocery aisle, picking up a few things for them to eat over the next few days. The result was that their cart was loaded by the time they were finished.

After checking out, Grayson hauled the groceries to the car first, then they each carried their respective bags into the public restrooms to change into dry clothing. She felt much better wearing dry clothes and running a brush through her damp hair. A shower would be nice, but she told herself not to worry about it and to count her blessings.

Being wet and drenched wasn't a crisis. Thanks to

Grayson's quick response, she'd survived when their boating mission could have ended much worse.

A wave of emotion hit hard, a hard lump forming in her throat. It wasn't good for her to be so dependent on Grayson Clark.

She cared about him, more deeply than she had ever cared for Andrew. He was sweet, smart, strong, and incredibly supportive.

And she had no idea how she'd move on with her life without him once the danger was over.

GRAYSON WAITED for Eve near the women's restroom. His wallet had been soaked, but at least his credit cards had worked.

No more delays or excuses, he silently lectured himself. Time to take Eve directly to the Ravenswood safe house. Where she belonged.

Every time she thanked him for keeping her safe, a new wave of guilt swamped him. Half the time, he was the one who'd placed her in the line of fire. And that had to stop.

No more taking her along on wild-goose chases.

When Eve finally emerged from the restroom, he could tell she was upset. "What's wrong?" He took the bag of wet clothing from her fingers. The good thing about the safe house was that there was a washer and dryer.

"Nothing." Her attempt to smile was pathetic. "I guess it's all catching up with me."

He slipped his arm around her shoulders. "I'm sorry for everything you've been through. You'll feel better once we get to the safe house."

"Yeah." She nodded half-heartedly. "I keep seeing

Geoff getting into that boat and wondering why he would do something like this."

He'd thought of that too. As much as he wanted to offer comfort, he knew they should get out of the store. It was, after all, a public place. And they'd spent more time there than he'd intended.

All because he'd wanted her to be comfortable.

"Let's go. We'll discuss various options of what Abbott has gotten mixed up in on the way."

"Sure." She rested her head against his chest for a moment, then straightened. "I'm ready."

"Good." He did his best to offer a reassuring smile. "Because I think the ice cream is melting out there."

That made her chuckle, as he'd hoped. He hugged her again and then bent his head to kiss her.

She turned into his arms, kissing him back with a level of intensity he hadn't anticipated. His heart swelled with love, but all too soon, she broke off from the kiss.

"Thank you," she whispered, and this time, he didn't feel any guilt at all.

"Any time," he managed, unable to hide a grin. They needed to hit the road, but he wouldn't have traded those past few minutes for anything. Having Eve in his arms after all these years was a gift he would cherish.

He told himself this was different from his relationship with Monica. It felt different, and while Eve had lived a protected life, she was stronger than she gave herself credit for.

After stowing their bags in the back seat, they climbed in. He started the engine and headed back to the interstate. The city of Peabody was farther from Milwaukee, which meant they had a good forty minutes of driving to reach the safe house.

"If these attacks are really about my research, I don't see why Geoff Abbott is involved," she said after a long moment. "His research is very different from mine."

"The only way it makes sense is if someone paid Geoff a significant amount of money." He glanced at her. "You saw those houses on Peabody Lake. The smallest one is bigger than two of mine."

She frowned. "But that's just it. Why pay money to get rid of me? What's the point?"

As she voiced her frustration, he noticed a gunmetal-gray SUV two cars behind him. They were too far away for him to see if there were any bullet holes or other damage to the vehicle. "Hold that thought. We may have company."

"Not again?" She twisted in her seat.

"Yes. Sit tight, I'm going to lose him." With that, he punched the gas and abruptly changed lanes, darting around two other vehicles to put distance between their rental and the gunmetal-gray SUV. There may be no point in checking with rental companies. If this was the same car, the driver of the vehicle hadn't returned it yet.

The gunmetal-gray SUV kept pace, also changing lanes, but surprisingly didn't try to close the gap. Was he wrong about the car? The color was right, but that didn't mean much. There was more than one gunmetal-gray SUV out there. Still, he couldn't afford to take a chance.

Maybe the ball-cap driver of the boat had seen Eve go into the water and figured they'd go to the closest department store to buy replacements.

He should have stopped at a place closer to the safe house, but it was too late to turn the clock back now. He sped up again, changed lanes, then swerved to cross three lanes of traffic to reach the closest exit.

As they left the freeway, he tried to get a glimpse of the

gunmetal-gray SUV. He thought he saw it drive past, not going fast or slow but keeping pace with the rest of the traffic. It was odd the driver didn't at least try to follow.

"We lost him?" Eve asked, glancing over her shoulder as if to make sure.

"For now." He honestly wasn't sure what to think. Had the vehicle been following them or not? If so, their rental was likely compromised, but they didn't have time to waste. They needed to get to Ravenswood ASAP, preferably without using the interstate.

The only good thing was that no one outside the police department and the few people who had used it in the past knew the location of the safe house. It would be impossible for anyone to find them there.

He tapped the screen of the computer system, bringing up the map app. He inputted their destination and waited for the app to provide him several ways to get there. He took a right-hand turn and headed southwest to a lesser-traveled highway. This route would take them much longer, but that was fine.

No more mistakes, he thought grimly. Maybe the gunmetal-gray SUV wasn't the same one who'd tailed them in the past. He may have overreacted over nothing.

Still, he kept a wary eye on the rearview mirror as he took the back roads to Ravenswood. He glanced at Eve to see she was watching traffic around them, too, turning occasionally in her seat to look behind them.

He was frustrated knowing how much danger she was in. And with that, his thoughts went right back to the incident on Peabody Lake. He didn't know the Peabody area well enough to guess at the addresses of the homes in the section they'd been in, but he made a mental note to pull up a map as soon as they were settled in the safe house.

The way the red-and-white boat had slowed down made him think they were about to pull into a specific place. He placed a call to Roscoe.

"Yo, what's up?" Roscoe asked.

"We're still en route to the safe house," he explained. "We're taking the long way after I caught a glimpse of a gunmetal-gray SUV on the interstate."

"Wow, I thought you would have been in Ravenswood by now," Roscoe said. "I'm at the precinct with Joe. He has Gabe Melrose tracking down a list of Peabody Lake property owners."

"Good. I have a feeling knowing who lives there will blow this case wide open."

"I hear you," Roscoe agreed. "Are you okay? Any other problems?"

"We're good. Just wanted to check in." He felt better knowing Roscoe, Joe, and the others would be working the case. Maybe it was time he left them to it and stayed focused on protecting Eve.

Not kissing her, he reminded himself sternly. *Protecting her*.

Two completely different things.

"It's really rural out here, isn't it?" Eve gestured to her window. "That must be a dairy farm."

"Yes." He arched a brow. "You do know that Wisconsin is known as the dairy state, right?"

"Well, yes, but I figured those farms were far away." She frowned. "I really need to get out more."

And wasn't that the understatement of the year? Somehow, he refrained from saying the words out loud. "When was the last time you took a vacation?" he asked instead.

She shrugged. "I attend research conferences. I've been to Seattle, Chicago, New York, and Atlanta."

"Okay, what sorts of tourist things did you do there? Go up in the Space Needle in Seattle? See the Statue of Liberty or a Broadway show in New York?"

"None of those things." She grimaced. "I took the subway—they call it the Marta—in Atlanta. That was interesting."

"That doesn't count." He found it incredibly sad that her idea of a vacation was a research conference. Especially since she hadn't done anything fun while spending time in some of the biggest cities in the country.

"I know you think I'm lame," she said in a low voice. "But I plan to make some changes to my life once things get back to normal."

He reached over to take her hand. "I'm glad to hear it. There's more to living than work. You deserve to have fun too."

"Yes, well, I guess I've let my work overtake my life." She squeezed his hand. "Other than attending church services, I don't socialize much. Well, I did with Andrew, but that was about it."

He was secretly glad she wasn't pining for the guy. Any man that would chase a woman like Bambi, rather than Eve, needed his head examined.

"Why aren't you seeing anyone, Grayson?"

Her question surprised him, although it shouldn't have. He hesitated, then decided it was time for her to know the truth. "I haven't dated anyone since Monica Wright. She—well, didn't take it well when I called things off."

She glanced at him with concern. "Did she stalk you?"

"No, that would have been better." He swallowed hard, then added, "She overdosed on her prescription medication."

Eve sucked in a harsh breath. "Oh, Grayson, I'm so sorry. But you must know that's not your fault."

"I'm not so sure." He'd tried to get past the guilt.

"She must have had some emotional issues prior to dating you to do something that drastic," Eve insisted.

"She was on antidepressants." He shrugged. "The point is that I haven't dated anyone in a long time."

"You just need to find the right woman," she insisted.

Was she referring to herself? And why did that thought give him hope?

Time to change the subject. "Interesting that Nick Strong never called you back."

"You think he was the driver of the boat." It wasn't a question.

"I don't know what to think." And that much was true. It felt like the investigation was stymied at every turn.

They drove in silence for a while. The nice thing about taking back highways was that it was easy to verify they weren't being followed. Oh there was some traffic, but not many vehicles and the driver almost always turned to head in another direction.

When he pulled up to the safe house, Eve looked at the building with frank curiosity. "It doesn't look like a safe house."

"What's a safe house supposed to look like?" He teased, putting the gear shift into park. "Trust me, the windows are bulletproof. That's the best part of the place."

"I'm not sure what I expected. It looks like any other neighborhood house." She pushed her door open and slid out. "I trust it's safe."

He opened the back hatch, then headed up to use the passcode on the door. Once he had it open, he returned for the groceries. The ice-cream container was on top, and he winced at how soft it was. Bummer. He had a weakness for ice cream.

Oh well, he shouldn't have indulged in something so juvenile anyway. They had bigger things to worry about.

It took three trips to get everything from the SUV into the safe house. Then, just to be extra cautious, he checked the vehicle for a tracking device. Finding nothing, he headed back inside to discover Eve had already started putting everything away. In moments, she had the kitchen neat as a pin, with the ingredients for their spaghetti dinner set aside on the counter. She glanced at him as he opened the bags of their wet clothes.

"What are you doing with those?"

"Washing them." He carried them into the small laundry room located down the hall near the bathroom. He took a moment to check the labels, then tossed them inside and added detergent.

When that task was finished, he returned to the kitchen to set up the computer. The first thing he did was pull up a map of Peabody Lake.

"That's where we were?" Eve leaned over his shoulder to peer at the screen. "It didn't look so long and narrow when we were on it."

"Lakes can be deceiving, especially since this one is rather large." Doing his best to ignore her nearness, he opened another window and typed in the name and address of the restaurant where they'd gotten the boat. Then he plotted it on the map, trying to imagine the route Roscoe had taken as they'd followed the red-and-white boat.

It was nearly impossible because he didn't have any other landmarks to go by. He thought it was generally in a diagonal direction, heading northwest. Using the restaurant address as a starting point, he mapped out the potential addresses of the homes where they'd caught up to the speedboat.

His phone rang, and seeing Roscoe's name on the screen, he quickly grabbed it. "Please tell me you have something to go on."

"We've got something, but it's not good," Roscoe said in a serious tone. "Geoff Abbott was pulled out of Lake Peabody in an apparent drowning. There's been no sign of the red-and-white boat either."

"A drowning." He caught Eve's anguished expression. "No way did he drown by accident."

"I agree with you there, the Peabody Police Department isn't convinced either, although they apparently see many drownings with people overindulging in alcoholic beverages. There was a bruise on the back of his head, which could mean he hit his head on the edge of the boat as he fell, or someone smacked him in the head before pushing him in." Roscoe sighed. "I just thought you should know. Whatever connection Geoff Abbott had in this has been effectively eliminated."

Just like Andrew Thomas, he thought. Although, they still had no evidence Andrew's murder was related to the attacks on Eve. While it was clear to him, Abbott's untimely demise was. Why else would ball-cap guy try to avoid them out on the lake? "What does Joe think?"

"He agrees with us that the timing is fishy, haha," Roscoe added.

Normally, he'd have chuckled at the lame joke. But things were going from bad to worse. "I don't suppose Gabe has found anything yet."

"He's still working on it. Oh wait." There was a pause as Roscoe spoke to someone. "Melrose came through big time. Guess who owns a house on Peabody Lake?"

"Don't keep me in suspense, Roscoe. Who?"

"Do you know a guy by the name of Dennis Powers? Apparently, he's one of the owners of a pharmaceutical company in Illinois."

"Owens and Powers Pharmaceuticals," he said in a dazed tone. "That's the company Bambi works for."

He turned to see Eve's gaze widen in horror as one big piece of the puzzle fell into place. This was the connection they'd needed between the attacks on Eve and Andrew Thomas's murder.

CHAPTER FOURTEEN

The twin assaults of hearing that Dennis Powers of O&P Pharmaceuticals owned a house on Peabody Lake and that Geoff Abbott had been found dead in the same lake hit her in the chest with the force of a locomotive going at full speed.

She couldn't breathe, could barely think. It was all too much.

Pressing a hand to her chest, she tried to calm her racing heart. It took a long moment for reality to sink in. Dennis Powers was likely the person behind these attacks.

Was likely the one who wanted her dead.

Why hadn't she realized this was all about money? If her research study was a success, she could dramatically cut the need for diabetes medications. Especially the newer, more expensive drugs that had recently hit the market.

She sank into the closest chair as a wave of sick realization washed over her. The pharmaceutical companies didn't want her to cure diabetes. Or to even substantially decrease the number of patients who suffered from the disease.

Because that would take money out of their own pocket.

"Thanks, Roscoe," she heard Grayson say. "Let me know how that goes."

She pulled herself together with an effort. "How what goes?"

"Joe is sending Flynn and Cassidy out to talk to Dennis Powers," he said. "They have his Peabody home address and hope to catch him there. If not, they'll work with the Chicago PD to meet him at his primary residence there."

"He owns two houses?" She sighed. "I guess I shouldn't be surprised. I always knew pharmaceutical companies brought in big bucks."

"Yes, exactly." He reached for her hands. "We have a good lead, Eve. Now that we know O and P is involved, I'm sure we'll get to the bottom of this mess very soon."

"I hope so." She gripped his hands tightly. "It hurts to know this is all about greed, Grayson. As if having two homes and a ton of money isn't enough, they want to eliminate the ability to cure a devastating disease. How cold, cruel, and callous is that?"

"Very," he agreed.

"And why kill Andrew? That doesn't make sense."

"Maybe Andrew uncovered something about O and P that he didn't like. We know Bambi has an alibi, but it could be a hammer was used on Andrew to divert suspicion to someone else."

His logic made sense, even if she had trouble comprehending this level of greed. "I'm sure Dennis Powers will deny any and all accusations and that he'll have high-priced lawyers on hand to represent him." She was already thinking several steps ahead. "What if the police can't prove he's responsible? What if he just goes free?"

"Let's try not to imagine the worst-case scenario." He offered a reassuring smile. "Trust the process. We know more now than we did before. Criminals generally make a few mistakes. I'm confident we'll find and capitalize on them."

"I hope you're right about that." It wasn't that she didn't have faith, she did. But she feared money and power would win out over those with as much clout behind them. "I feel terrible about Geoff. I don't believe he would have willingly done anything to hurt me."

"I get the sense he was dragged into this somehow," Grayson agreed. After a long pause, he asked, "We need to consider your boss a suspect."

"Roger?" She wanted to protest, but after everything that had happened, she knew Grayson was right. "I'm not sure how it helps him to get rid of me. I don't think they can keep the five-million research grant if I'm dead."

"Maybe Dennis Powers is paying him far more than that. I'm sure O and P Pharmaceuticals is worth millions, maybe even billions dollars."

She shrugged, battling a wave of helplessness. They were talking about numbers so big she couldn't comprehend them. And who needed billions of dollars anyway? It was inconceivable that any one person should have that much. Not that she begrudged hard work and dedication for a financial reward, but to resort to violence to keep it was despicable.

That money should be put to better use rather than lining the pockets of the CEOs and owners.

"I want this horrible nightmare to end, Grayson." She suddenly felt overwhelmingly exhausted. "It seems as if we've been on the run forever, and I just want it to end."

"I know, and we'll get there." He stood and tugged her upright. Then he drew her into his arms. "I'm here for you, Eve."

"I know." She buried her face against his chest, grateful for his strength and never-ending support. She would never have survived all of this without him.

He smoothed a hand down her back as if comforting a child. Too bad her feelings for him were far different from that. She wanted him to kiss her the way he had before. As if he found her as attractive as the other women in his life.

Yeah, and maybe she'd make a billion dollars in her lifetime too. *Not.*

Squeezing her eyes shut, she clung to him, wishing she never had to let him go. But she also knew he wasn't interested, after the way his relationship with Monica had ended so badly.

"Eve?" He stroked his hand down her back again. "Are you okay? Please don't cry."

"I'm not." Her voice was muffled against his chest, and she hadn't been crying until he'd mentioned it. Now tears burned her eyelids. She sniffled and blinked them back with an effort, reluctantly lifting her head from his chest. "Sorry, didn't mean to fall apart on you like that."

"I'm not sorry." He tucked a damp strand of her hair behind her ear. "I care about you, Eve."

Their gazes clung for a long moment before he slowly lowered his mouth to hers. She could have avoided the kiss if she'd wanted to, but she met him halfway, telling herself this may be her last chance to kiss him like this.

He caught her close, deepening their embrace. Desire sizzled in her blood, making her head swim. Grayson could have any woman he wanted, but here in this brief moment he was hers.

She prayed the kiss would never end, but of course, his phone rang. He broke off the kiss, taking a moment to rest his forehead against hers as he struggled to breathe, before stepping back to pick the device up from the table.

"Yeah?" His voice was low and husky, and his rugged smile made her stomach flip. Then his expression hardened. "He must have been there recently, otherwise where was the ball-cap guy taking Abbott?"

They were talking about Dennis Powers. Her thrill over kissing Grayson faded fast. They didn't know for sure Dennis was guilty, but she already despised him.

Which wasn't fair, she knew. God would not want her to wallow in hate.

"Okay, fine. I don't like it, but I know you're doing your best." Grayson lowered his phone and raked a hand through his hair. "No sign of Powers at the Peabody Lake house. They think he's probably still on the road, though, heading back to Chicago, so they're going to try to catch up with him there."

"I hope they do." She tried to sound positive, even though it felt as if the odds were stacked against them. An awkward silence fell between them in the wake of their embrace. For a moment, Grayson looked as if he wanted to say something, but he glanced at the computer instead.

"I need to see if we can tie the rental car to O and P Pharmaceuticals." He dropped into the closest chair. "The more evidence we can get the better. Lining up the details can only help our case against them."

She nodded, moving toward the kitchen. "I'll start dinner." She wasn't the best cook on the planet, but she could follow a recipe. And this was a meal she'd made often enough that she didn't need one.

As she browned the ground beef, she thought again of Geoff Abbott. Had the man in the ball cap driving the boat been Nick Strong? Had both men taken their resentment against her to a new and drastic level? She could imagine Geoff wanting out of whatever Nick was planning, only to be killed as a result.

She shivered, thinking about how Geoff had died so soon after they'd followed him across the lake. Falling off the boat wearing a life jacket wasn't the same thing, but for several seconds, she'd feared she would drown too.

Looking through the window above the kitchen sink, she stared at the clear blue summer sky and prayed that God would continue to watch over her and Grayson.

And she made a silent promise to let Grayson know how much she loved him before their time together was over.

THE WORK WAS TEDIOUS, but Grayson kept at it, going to each rental car company and asking about a gunmetal-gray SUV that may have been returned with a bullet hole. Each time he made the call, he had to wait for someone to get a manager. It was something he should have anticipated since the average desk clerk would not want to be the one to share something like that.

And may not even know about a damaged vehicle.

After each conversation, he left his name and phone number, requesting a call back if such a damaged vehicle was returned. At least none of the managers gave him a hard time about that. Seems as if being a party to a crime, even inadvertently, was enough to ensure cooperation.

He was on his fourth company when Roscoe called. He picked up the phone, praying for good news. "What's up, Roscoe?"

"We had the Chicago PD head to Powers's home; he's

not there. We have his car registration and license plate number, but he hasn't gone through the Illinois state tollways yet."

Grayson had a bad feeling about this. "Does this guy own other properties? Either out of state or out of the country?" The thought of Powers disappearing for a while down in the Cayman Islands or some other tax-sheltered place made his blood boil. Yet Powers was also the sort who would not get his own hands dirty.

He'd hire people to do that for him.

Like the ball-cap guy and maybe even others. He didn't want to jump to conclusions, but had a feeling that Nick Strong was the driver of the boat. And the one who'd pushed Geoff Abbott overboard.

Proof, he reminded himself. Speculation was useless. They needed proof.

"I have Melrose working on that now," Roscoe said, interrupting his thoughts. "But if this guy is smart, he'll have that information buried deep."

"I'm calling rental car companies but so far have not found the gunmetal SUV with a bullet hole. I saw a similar vehicle on the road behind us after leaving Peabody, but I lost it. Could be nothing or it may mean the shooter is still using the rental."

"It feels like we're spinning our wheels," Roscoe admitted. "I was hoping the BOLO for Nick Strong would yield results by now."

"Not if he's with Dennis Powers, flying who knows where." He wondered if the billionaire would take Strong with him or get rid of him, too, the way Strong had eliminated Abbott.

Which is all pure speculation, he reminded himself. He needed to stay on track.

"That's true," Roscoe agreed. "We don't have enough evidence for a search warrant for his financials, so there's no way to know if he's purchased a plane ticket out of Milwaukee or hired a private jet. What I can do is to head back to O'Dell's Pub to see if I can figure out if Geoff Abbott said anything to the bartender or other patrons there. Maybe he hinted at the trouble he's in."

"Good. Let me know how that goes." He wished he could join Roscoe in questioning the pub patrons, but he knew his place was here, keeping Eve safe. "I'll call if I find anything on the rental car."

"Understood. Later." Roscoe ended the call.

"Any update?" Eve asked, turning from the stove to look at him.

"Not really." He didn't want her to be depressed by the lack of progress; he was feeling lousy enough for the both of them. "Something smells good."

She smiled. "Dinner will be ready in fifteen minutes."

He glanced at his watch, surprised it was past five thirty. Earlier than he usually ate dinner, but after the day they'd had, he was hungry enough not to complain. "Thanks. That sounds good."

"I found root beer in the fridge," she said. "It must have been left behind by whoever was here last. The ice cream was pretty melted, but we can make root beer floats."

He chuckled. "I haven't had one of those since I was a kid. But I thought soda has too many chemicals?"

"We'll make an exception." She turned back to the stove. "Finish up what you're doing and set the table."

"One last call." He wasn't sure how late some of these rental car managers would work. Nine to five? Ten to six? He didn't want to miss the opportunity. He dialed the number displayed on the computer screen and waited. The person who answered sounded harried.

He identified himself as an MPD officer. "I'm investigating a shooting that involved a gunmetal-gray SUV that we have reason to believe is a rental. Did you get a damaged vehicle returned recently matching that description? There would likely be a bullet hole in the vehicle's windshield."

"A bullet hole? No, we haven't had anything like that." There was a pause before the guy said, "Looks like we do have a gunmetal-gray SUV that was supposed to be returned today at noon but hasn't come in yet."

Grayson's pulse quickened. "Can you tell me who rented it?"

"I'm not supposed to give you that information without a warrant," the clerk said. "But if you give me your name and number, I'll call you if the vehicle is returned with damage that resembles a bullet hole. That's pretty serious, and we would always cooperate with an ongoing investigation."

The compromise was better than nothing. And he'd reach out to Rhy to get the warrant. "I appreciate that. Call as soon as you get it."

"I will. And you should know that if we don't hear from the person renting the car within twenty-four hours, our policy is to report the vehicle as stolen. In that case, we'd give you the renter's name, address, and other information."

"Great. Thanks for that." He ended the call, feeling certain he'd found the correct rental car company. He placed a call to Rhy about obtaining a warrant, and he promised to see if he could get one. With that task completed, he walked to the cupboard to get plates, cups, silverware, and napkins, convinced they were one step closer to finding out who shot at them.

"You found something?" Eve asked as she pulled garlic bread from the oven. It was store-bought but smelled delicious.

"Maybe. There's a gunmetal-gray SUV that was due back today at noon but hasn't been returned yet. Rhy's going to try to get a warrant for the name and address of the person who rented it."

She nodded as she brought a bowl of meat sauce and noodles to the table. "You think it's the one that was following us earlier."

"No way to say for sure, but the delay could be related to the fact that the job hasn't been completed." At her confused look, he added, "Let's say the shooter was paid to eliminate you. He hasn't done that, so he can't return the vehicle until he has."

"I guess that makes sense." She looked glum as she brought the garlic bread to the table. "I think the best thing we can do right now is to pray."

"I've been praying a lot over the past few hours," he admitted, reaching over to clasp her hand. "I didn't realize the power of prayer until recently. I always feel better afterward, as if God has calmed my fears."

Her smile lit up her face. "I feel the same way. There's a Bible passage from Isaiah that always calls to me, it helps reassure me when I need to feel Him the most." She hesitated, gauging his reaction. When he nodded for her to continue, she said, "'Fear thou not; for I am with thee: be not dismayed; for I am thy God: I will strengthen thee; yea, I will help thee; yea, I will uphold thee with the right hand of my righteousness'" (Isaiah 41:10).

"That's beautiful," he murmured, touched by the words. He was humbled by how easily she was able to quote the Bible. "I can't say that I know a single Bible verse, but there is one that I heard about having no fear upon walking through the valley of the shadow of death. That's something that seems to happen while I'm on the job." He didn't want her to know how many tight spots he and his fellow officers had been in over the past two years.

"That's from Psalm twenty-three, another of my favorites." She reached over to touch his hand. "I don't know how you face danger every day, Grayson. It must take a special type of courage and dedication to do your job. I'll be keeping you in my prayers every day from now on. And now, we need to pray so we can eat." She bowed her head. "Dear Lord Jesus, we thank You for this food we are about to eat. We also thank You for keeping us safe in Your loving arms. Please grant us the strength and guidance we need to seek justice to those who would cause harm to innocent people. Amen."

"Amen." He reluctantly released her hand to pass her the noodles. "Ladies first."

"Thanks." It didn't take long for them to fill their plates with food. And he realized how important it was to thank God for their blessings. He had never gone hungry, but his work as a Milwaukee cop exposed him to those who had. He thought about how happy he was for Raelyn and her new fiancé, Pastor Isaiah Washington, especially after they had taken in a foster son who also knew what it was like to go hungry.

Was that something he could do one day? Maybe. If Eve was up for that.

Whoa, Eve? What was he thinking? They hadn't even discussed anything beyond the case. Two kisses did not equal a relationship. For a moment, he thought of Monica, then forced the image away.

Eve wasn't Monica. He probably should have realized

Monica was a little unstable before asking her out. But Eve was also going through a difficult time. Anything that developed between them now, might fizzle and die once their respective lives got back to normal. From what he could tell, Eve didn't appear to love the idea of his being a cop.

"Did your officers ever find Larry Kimmel?" she asked, jolting him from his thoughts.

It was a good question. And one that reminded him to stay focused on the case, not on the prospect of seeing Eve again on a personal level once this was over. "No, Roscoe didn't mention anything about him. After they discovered Geoff Abbott's body, I think they stayed focused on Nick Strong."

"That makes sense." She nibbled on her garlic bread.

"Not really." He reached for his phone and sent Roscoe a text asking about Larry Kimmel. "The fact is that everyone is considered a suspect until they've been cleared. And that includes Kimmel."

"That must be a horrible way to live," she said with a frown. "Always thinking the worst of people."

"It's not always easy. But having preconceived notions about a person's guilt or innocence will derail an investigation." He finished his spaghetti with a sigh of appreciation. "Thanks, that was really good."

"You're welcome." She rose reaching for his empty plate. "Root beer floats coming up."

He chuckled at that, glancing at his phone when Roscoe responded to his message. *Yes, spoke to L. K. He's clear. Not a suspect.*

Ok, thanks.

Despite his recent lecture about keeping an open mind, he wasn't necessarily surprised that Kimmel was clean. His gut was telling him Nick Strong was the guy they were looking for.

And they needed to find him very soon.

The sound of a phone buzzing made him frown. Eve patted her pockets, then rose to cross over to the kitchen counter.

"Wait! Don't answer it!" He jumped to his feet.

It was too late. "Hello?" Her brow furrowed as she listened to the caller on the other end of the line. "Slow down, I can't figure out what you're saying." Another pause, then, "Okay, but what makes you think Geoff Abbott wants to hurt you? I can reassure you that Geoff isn't out there because, unfortunately, he's dead."

He did not like the sound of this. Two long strides had him crossing the room to join her. It was all he could do not to yank the phone from her fingers. "Let me talk to him."

She nodded. "Yes, I'm sure of that. Listen, I have police officer Grayson Clark right here. Talk to him, I promise he'll get officers over to your place right away. Here he is." She finally handed him the phone.

"Officer Clark speaking. Who is this?" he asked.

There was nothing but silence.

"Are you there?" he demanded. He turned toward Eve, but she was heading over to the door.

There was still nothing but silence on the other end of the line. A warning chill washed over him. "Eve? Don't go outside . . ."

She paused in the act of opening the door. Then a booted heel punched the door, pushing her backward and sending her stumbling against the wall. His phone jangled with notifications from the security system outside, but too late to do him any good.

A man came into the room, holding a small yet lethal

gun. Not Nick Strong as he'd expected, but someone else. He frantically searched his memory, the name Dave Firestein finally clicking as Eve spoke.

"Dave, what are you doing? How did you find us here?" Eve pushed herself upright from the wall, gaping at the armed man.

"I need to finish this." His gaze was locked on Eve but then quickly turned to him. "Don't move, Clark. Reach for that gun and I'll shoot you too."

It was hard to believe a man who held a PhD and dedicated his life to research was comfortable handling a weapon, but there was no doubt in his mind that Firestein had used the gun before.

And would not hesitate to use it again.

"You don't want to do this," Grayson said, adopting a reasonable tone. He still had Eve's phone in his hand, and he lowered it to his side as he punched in the numbers for Roscoe's cell. "We already know Dennis Powers of O and P Pharmaceuticals is the one who hired you. They don't want Eve to succeed in her research, right? So they asked for your help to get rid of her. You scheduled the live-streaming presentation."

Firestein's gaze flickered between him and Eve, almost as if confirming that Grayson had gotten this much right.

"If you agree to cooperate with us in nailing Powers, I promise to work with the DA's office to make sure you don't get any jail time."

"Yeah, right," Firestein sneered.

"I'm not lying to you. My boss, Rhy Finnegan, has a brother-in-law and a cousin who both work in the DA's office. Rhy has a lot of clout there, enough to make sure you walk away from this unscathed." It was a rash promise that he couldn't necessarily deliver on but decided it would be better to ask forgiveness later. Right now, he needed to get that weapon out of Firestein's hands. "Please, put the gun down. It's over. We're going to nail Powers, so there's no point in doing this. No reason to kill an innocent woman."

"I don't want to," Firestein admitted. "But I agreed to do my part. I'm sorry, Eve. I need you to come with me."

"Okay." To his horror, she eased toward the door. "I'll go with you, Dave. Just you and me, okay? Leave Grayson out of this."

"No!" He couldn't believe she would leave with this guy. Firestein abruptly fired in his direction, sending him diving to the floor, rolling, and coming up with his own weapon in hand.

But they were already out the door.

He prayed as he sprang to his feet to rush after them.

CHAPTER FIFTEEN

He'd shot Grayson! Eve winced at how hard Dave gripped her arm, dragging her relentlessly toward the gunmetal-gray SUV. The warmth of the sun didn't reach the coldness in her heart. She'd gone with Dave to protect Grayson, but that hadn't worked.

"Why don't you just shoot me now?" she demanded, instinctively dragging her feet. Maybe Grayson wasn't hurt that bad. Maybe he had been able to call for backup.

Maybe there was still a way out of this!

"I have strict instructions to bring you to a specific location about ten miles from here," Dave said. "Let's go!"

That didn't make any sense. Dave could easily shoot her and Grayson here at the safe house without anyone being the wiser.

The gunmetal-gray SUV was parked on the street just yards away, and she suddenly knew they should not get inside. She stopped walking, allowing all her weight to sag toward the ground.

"What are you doing?" Dave hissed. "Get up! Move it! We're going in the car!"

"No. I think there's a bomb planted beneath it." She was almost on her knees now, looking up at Dave frantically. "You know they killed Geoff Abbott, right? I think there's a bomb beneath that vehicle to take us both out of the equation."

"That's ridiculous," Dave spat. But then he slowed his pace, eyeing the SUV warily. From behind him, she was thrilled to see Grayson coming out of the house then. Upon seeing the weapon he held in both hands, she ducked her head to make herself a smaller target.

"Drop the weapon now!" Grayson barked. A nanosecond later, he fired.

She felt Dave's body jolt from the impact of the bullet striking flesh and bone. Then his body slumped against her, nearly crushing her onto the driveway. She did her best to roll out from underneath him, but the angle was such that she couldn't quite manage it. She was folded in half like an accordion.

Finally, the weapon dropped from his fingers, hitting the concrete with a thud. Then Grayson was there, kicking the gun out of reach and dragging the injured man off her. "Eve? Are you okay? You're not hurt?"

"I'm fine." She silently thanked God for sparing her life and Grayson's. "He didn't shoot."

Sirens split the air as a squad pulled up behind the gunmetal-gray SUV. Roscoe jumped out from behind the wheel, bringing a wave of relief.

But then she pushed herself to her feet. "You need to get the squad away from the SUV," she said. "I think there might be a bomb inside."

Grayson and Roscoe both looked at her as if she'd lost her marbles. "It's okay, Eve. You're safe now," Grayson said in a soothing voice.

"I know, thanks to you." She met Grayson's gaze. "But I'm telling you, there must be a reason Dave was instructed to take me somewhere. He could have shot us both and left, but that wasn't what he'd been told to do. I think the plan was to eliminate me and Dave at the same time. Please, Grayson. Check the SUV for a bomb." She would do it herself if she had a clue what to look for.

Yet something was telling her they didn't have much time.

Grayson and Roscoe glanced at each other and shrugged. "She has a point about why he'd try to take her out of here," Roscoe said. "That only made it easier for you to nail him."

Dave let out a low groan, clutching his shoulder. "He shot me."

She almost told him he deserved it but managed to hold her tongue. Dropping to her knees beside him, she examined his wound. She was no medical doctor, but it looked to be high enough to have missed his heart, but may have hit his lung.

"We need an ambulance," she called. Grayson lifted his hand to acknowledge her comment as he and Roscoe approached the SUV. They each took one side, kneeling, then lying on their backs to examine the undercarriage.

"She's right! There is a bomb!" Grayson shouted. "We need to get out of here now!"

"What?" Dave looked confused. "What's he talking about?"

"Come on, you need to stand." She grabbed his arm on his uninjured side and tried to tug him upright. "We can't stay here. That thing could blow any minute."

The sense of urgency was stronger now. She couldn't help thinking that the device was set to detonate within a specific time frame. He'd been told to take her to a location that wasn't that far away. Maybe that was when it was set to go off.

Apparently, hearing about the bomb gave Dave Firestein the strength he needed to get up from the driveway. She slid her arm around his waist, trying to support him as they hobbled farther away from the SUV.

Grayson and Roscoe ran toward them too. Roscoe took Dave off her hands, half carrying the injured man as they headed down the road. Grayson wrapped his strong arms around her. "Hurry," he urged.

They managed to get halfway down the street, roughly fifty yards from the safe house, when the loud explosion rocked the earth. She would have fallen if not for Grayson holding on to her. She felt the heat of the blast against her back as they kept going down the street, putting as much distance between them and the gunmetal-gray SUV as possible.

"A bomb. There was a bomb," Dave muttered over and over as if he still couldn't comprehend what had happened.

"I told you that." She couldn't explain how she knew; maybe God had given her the wisdom she'd needed at just the right moment. It was the only explanation she could come up with as to how she'd known.

This nightmare had started with a bomb. They should have anticipated it might end with one too.

"How did you know?" Grayson asked, stopping when they were far enough away from the blast. The gunmetal-gray SUV was on fire now, flames flickering up to the sky.

"I just did." Her stomach knotted as she watched the remnants of the vehicle burn to ash. Then she turned into Grayson's arms. "I'm so glad you weren't hurt. I was afraid Dave had shot you."

"He missed, but not by much," Grayson said with a frown. He glared at Dave. "You should have cooperated with us."

"I didn't know about the bomb," Dave babbled. "I didn't know!"

"That's because you're an idiot," she said wearily. "I told you Geoff Abbott was murdered. You should have expected the same would happen to you."

"I agree with Eve; it appears that Powers doesn't like loose ends," Roscoe drawled. "Is he the one who hired you?"

"Yes, he hired me," Dave said, accepting his defeat. "But there's someone else you should look at."

Eve sighed. "Nick Strong."

Dave looked surprised. "Yes, but how did you know?"

"We know more than you think. But how did you get involved in this?" Grayson asked.

Dave looked chagrined. "I'm on the board of directors for O and P pharmaceuticals."

Grayson scowled and reached for his phone. She listened as he filled Rhy in on what had just gone down.

"How were you found at the safe house?" From where she stood beside Grayson, she could hear Rhy's incredulous tone.

"I'm not sure. There's no GPS on the rental. Maybe they traced Eve's disposable cell number, or they had two cars following and I didn't realize it." Grayson didn't sound happy as he offered the two suggestions. "We need a ride out of here ASAP. And Dave Firestein needs medical attention."

"Flynn and Cassidy are on the way, and I'll send an ambulance too."

"Thanks." Grayson ended the call. He pressed a kiss to the top of her head. "I think it may finally be over."

She nodded, leaning against him. As happy as she was about the nightmare being over, she didn't want to let Grayson go.

SCANNING THE AREA, still on high alert, Grayson hugged Eve close, wishing he could tell her how much he loved her. Yet the sirens in the distance indicated both the ambulance and likely the local police were on the way. The explosion would have been called in by someone living nearby.

He still couldn't believe she was right about the presence of a bomb. If Firestein had managed to get her shoved into the vehicle quickly enough to take off, they would both be dead.

It was horrifying to know how close he'd come to losing Eve. He continued holding her, even as the ambulance and local police pulled up next to them.

Roscoe was in uniform, complete with his badge. He stepped forward, dragging Firestein with him. "MPD officers Jones and Clark. We have a perp by the name of David Firestein in custody; he's injured and needs transport to Trinity Medical Center."

"What happened here?" the officer demanded.

Grayson sighed, wishing he could just leave and get Eve out of there. The immediate danger was over, but he wouldn't rest until he'd gotten Strong and Powers in custody.

Especially Powers. The rest of the research scientists were pawns in this deadly game.

He abruptly turned to Firestein. "Where's Nick Strong?"

Firestein averted his gaze. "I don't know, but I was supposed to meet him with Eve at the park."

So Strong had been targeted for elimination too. But he probably didn't realize that yet. "I need you to call him."

"What's in it for me?" Firestein asked. "You said your boss has connections in the DA's office."

It was all he could do not to punch the guy in the face. "Yeah, okay. I'll put in a good word for you. Call him. Explain you've been delayed but will be bringing Eve to the designated meeting spot." As he spoke, Flynn and Cassidy arrived; thankfully, Flynn was driving his personal SUV.

"Ah, okay." Firestein finally relented, reaching for his phone. Giving Eve over to Cassidy, he grabbed Firestein's arm and gestured for Flynn to follow him. He half carried the injured man far enough away from the others so they wouldn't be heard as background noise.

"Hurry," Grayson urged, knowing the firetrucks would be sounding their arrival any minute. "Let him know you're in a different car, a black SUV. Tell him the other one died on the side of the road."

After fumbling for his phone, Firestein made the call. "I have her, we're on the way, but I had to get a different car, the other one died on me." There was a pause as the professor listened for a moment, then he said, "Yes, we'll be there in ten minutes."

"Where?" Grayson demanded when he ended the call.

"Greenland Park near the restrooms." Firestein looked pale, his strength wanning.

He gestured for Roscoe to join them. "Take him in the ambulance. Keep an eye on Eve, Flynn and I are heading out."

"Wait!" Eve pulled out of Cassidy's grip. "If this

meeting is about me, I need to be there. Nick may take off if he doesn't see me."

He hesitated. To his surprise, Flynn nodded. "She's right. We'll keep her safe. I have a vest in the back of the car."

"Fine. Let's hit it." He silently prayed he wasn't making a mistake by bringing Eve with him.

"I can't believe how many of them are in this," Eve said from the back seat. Flynn was speeding through the subdivision, forced to go a different route as the firetrucks had indeed arrived. "Dave, Nick, and Geoff. All three of them!"

"Remember Geoff Abbott didn't look as if he'd gone along with the plan voluntarily," he said, trying to reassure her. "That's probably why Nick killed him."

"Still, how could they all be so blind to what Powers is doing?" She clearly wasn't buying it, her voice vibrated with despair. "He's against everything we do. Everything we stand for. Medical research is supposed to be about curing diseases, not capitalizing on sick people."

Hard to argue that point.

Flynn apparently agreed as he sped through the streets to reach their destination. When they were a mile away, Grayson said, "We both can't be in the car. Let me off here and I'll sneak around to approach him from behind."

"Got it." Flynn nodded his agreement to the plan as he pushed open the passenger door. "Be safe, bro."

"You too. Keep Eve out of danger."

"I should sit up front, don't you think?" Eve asked. Without waiting for an answer, she jumped out of the car and threw herself into his arms. "I love you, Grayson. Please don't get hurt."

His heart swelled, even though he knew it was probably

just the situation that had caused her to say that. "I love you too. I'll be fine. We're going to get him."

She kissed him, then pulled away to climb into the passenger seat. Feeling infused with strength and purpose, he darted across the grassy parkland, knowing exactly where to go. Thankfully, he and the rest of the team were somewhat familiar with the park.

He zigzagged through trees, slowing his pace when he caught a glimpse of the back side of the restroom building. He stealthily approached the back of the building, keeping his head down and his weapon in hand.

As he eased along the side of the building closest to the trees, he spotted a vehicle parked out front. The angle was such that he couldn't see the driver.

When he reached the corner of the building, he went down on one knee to peer around the corner. The SUV appeared empty except for the driver who had a baseball hat on. It wasn't easy to see the man's facial features, but he was certain the driver was Nick Strong. And that no one else was in the car.

Good, he thought. *Less potential for collateral damage.*

Flynn and Eve rolled slowly toward the parking lot. The moment Strong looked in his rearview mirror, Grayson sprang forward, rushing the SUV, and then tried to wrench open the driver's side door.

It was locked. He lifted his gun, pressing the muzzle against the window. "Drop your weapon and open the door! Now!"

When Nick hesitated, he fired through the glass, aiming for the headrest. The man let out a panicked shout and lifted both of his hands in surrender.

Punching his elbow through the window, Grayson reached in, unlocked the door, and wrenched it open. "Nick

Strong, you're under arrest for murder, attempted murder, and any other charges that we deem appropriate."

In the end, it was easier than he'd anticipated to get Nick Strong into custody. The professor glared at Eve as if this were all her fault.

Grayson thrust Strong toward Flynn, who cuffed him and continued reading him his rights.

It was finally over. Or would be once they had Powers in custody.

Eve opened the passenger-side door and rushed toward him. He caught her in his arms, crushing her close. "I love you," she whispered.

One declaration could be ignored, but to hear it twice? He forced himself to loosen his grip long enough to look down into her eyes. "You've been through a lot. Let's get you home, then we can talk."

The light in her gray eyes dimmed, but she nodded. "I'd like nothing more than to go home."

He kissed her cheek, then turned her back to the SUV. Since Flynn had Nick Strong in the back seat, he put Eve up front before climbing in beside their prisoner.

"How could you do it, Nick?" Eve turned in her seat to face her colleague. "How could you sell out to a pharmaceutical company?"

Strong glared at her. "You think you're so smart," he sneered. "What's a five-million-dollar grant compared to twenty million in cold hard cash in my pocket?"

"You have the right to remain silent," Grayson reminded him. "If I were you, I'd shut up. Besides, we already have Firestein in custody, and he's given us you and Powers on a silver platter."

"Oh, and you should know that the SUV Dave was driving blew up," Eve said. "Powers planned to kill you, me, and Dave with the car bomb, keeping that twenty million all to himself."

The color drained from Strong's face. Then he abruptly faced Grayson. "I'll tell you everything I know."

"Figured you would," Grayson agreed. "But we're not doing that until you've been processed through the system and provided legal counsel. I'm not having your confession thrown out over a lack of due process. And Firestein has first dibs on making a deal anyway."

Strong slumped against the door, as the amount of trouble he was in hit him like a sledgehammer. *Which is good*, Grayson thought. It was about time.

Strong and the others had been foolish to trust someone as amoral and downright evil as Dennis Powers. But that was what happened when you allowed greed to overrule basic common sense.

The rest of the trip to their precinct was done in silence. He gladly allowed Flynn to take Strong inside, not caring which of them got credit for the arrest. He was just thankful Eve wasn't harmed and that he could finally take her home.

He borrowed a vehicle from Joe Kingsley. The trip to Eve's house didn't take long. She didn't say anything, and he kept shooting her concerned glances, wondering what was going through her mind.

Did she regret saying she loved him? He knew some people used the word love loosely, like something they'd say to a friend.

Not someone they'd fallen in love with.

The way he'd fallen in love with her.

She was still unusually quiet when he pulled into the driveway. She opened her car door, then groaned.

"I forgot my bag with my notes back at the safe house."

"I'll make sure you get it back when they've finished processing the crime scene," he promised.

"Yeah." She looked upset for a moment, then shrugged. "It doesn't matter. I'm too tired to recreate my research notes now."

"You were going to work?" He shook his head. "No, you really need to rest and recover from all of this."

"You're right." She attempted a smile as they walked up to her garage door. She punched in the key code, revealing her bright-blue SUV.

Inside, her house looked exactly as they'd left it, after bringing Dottie in to assist with dismantling the bomb. She crossed over to drop onto the sofa. He sat beside her, deciding it would not be smart to leave her alone.

"Would you like something to drink?" He wasn't good at this sort of thing. "I can make coffee or tea."

"No, I'm fine." This time, her smile reached her eyes. "Thanks for saving my life. Again."

"You did the same for me." Something that still irked him. But now wasn't the time to chastise her. In truth, he'd been touched by her efforts to save him. "I think it's better if I sleep on your sofa tonight. In case you have nightmares."

"Oh, Grayson." To his shock and horror, tears filled her eyes. "That's so sweet."

"I-uh . . ." He had no idea what to say, so he simply drew her into his arms. "What am I going to do with you?" he murmured against her hair.

"Kiss me?" She lifted her watery gaze to his. "I love you, Grayson, but I understand you don't feel the same way. Or that you're not interested in being involved after what happened with your former girlfriend. But one last kiss would be nice."

"Hey, I do love you." He'd told her that, hadn't he?

"Eve, you're the smartest, prettiest, and kindest woman I know." He scowled. "Don't compare me to that idiot former boyfriend of yours."

She searched his gaze for a moment. "Okay, I won't do that if you won't compare me to Monica."

He sighed and nodded. "Okay, you're right. I have been trying to ignore my feelings for you. But even without Monica, I want you to know I've changed from the guy I was in high school." He offered a crooked smile. "I wanted to date you back then, but you didn't look at me twice. Put me in my place if you want to know the truth."

"Oh, Grayson." She swiped at her tears and smiled. "You're such a goof. Of course I was attracted to you, but I wasn't going to stand in line either."

"I'm glad you didn't because I think God waited all these years to bring us together for a reason. Because we needed to be older and wiser. I think we are right where we are supposed to be."

"You really believe that?" Her eyes were wide with hope.

"Yes, I do." He decided to fulfill her request to kiss her. He captured her mouth with his, hoping this would show her better than his attempt at poetic words, how much he cared.

She melted against him, kissing him back in a way that made his heart soar. Maybe she was telling him how she felt, too, without words.

It was a long time before they came up for air. He didn't want to let her go, but his phone was buzzing in his pocket.

"I'm sorry. I have to answer this." He glanced at the screen, noting Rhy's name. "Hey, boss. I hope you have good news."

"We found a partial print at Andrew Thomas's condo

that links Nick Strong to his murder. We picked up Bambi again, and she finally admitted to telling Andrew that Eve's research had to stop as it would impact their sales. Andrew defended Eve, which did not make Bambi happy. After the bombing, Andrew called Bambi demanding to know if she or the company was behind it. She denied it, but as we know, Andrew ended up murdered as a result. We believe the hammer was used to make it look unrelated to the attacks against Eve."

"I guess it's nice to know Andrew wasn't on board with the plan to derail Eve's research," he admitted.

"Yeah. Unfortunately, Powers is still on the loose," Rhy said. "I've called my brother Brady with the FBI to get federal resources to help us find him."

"That's good, he can't hide forever, right?" He tugged Eve closer so that her head rested on his chest. "Did you get anything useful from Firestein?"

"He gave us some information before they rushed him off to surgery. According to Bax, Strong keeps asking for a lawyer so he can make a deal too. Unfortunately, Strong is already looking at murder, but at least they're both ready and willing to turn on Dennis Powers."

"That's good. All we have to do is to find him." He said we, meaning the police, but he had no intention of leaving Eve. "I need some personal time, boss."

"Oh yeah?" He could almost imagine Rhy grinning on the other end of the phone. "Let me guess, you want to spend some time with the pretty doc?"

"As much time as she'll give me, yes." He smiled down at her. "Besides, I won't be convinced she's completely safe until Powers has been arrested."

"I hear you. Fine, take your time off, even though summer is our busiest time of year," Rhy groused.

"Thanks." He felt a twinge of regret leaving his team-mates shorthanded but knew that both Rhy and Joe would pitch in. Despite their ranks of captain and lieutenant respectively, both men preferred to have boots on the ground, helping out. "Call me as soon as you find Powers."

"Will do. Say hi to Eve for me." Rhy laughed prior to ending the call.

"Good grief," Eve whispered, pressing her face against his chest. "I feel like he was watching us kiss or something."

"No, but Rhy knows what it's like to fall in love." He bent to kiss her again. "And for the first time in my life, so do I. I love you, Eve."

"I love you too." She hugged him close, and he was thankful God had blessed him with the right woman at exactly the right time.

Three weeks later . . .

Eve was so engrossed in her research that she didn't hear Grayson come in until he drew her chair from the desk and hauled her into his arms, swinging her around so her feet left the ground. "We found him!"

She sucked in a harsh breath. "Dennis Powers?"

"Yes. With the feds' help, they were finally able to grab him up in a private resort in Canada." He kissed her. "That's the end of it. Based on the testimony of Fierstein and Strong, he won't see the light of day for a long time."

"What about other evidence against him?" She and Grayson had discussed how well Powers had covered his tracks, tricking the professors to do his bidding so that his hands were clean. "What if their testimony isn't enough?"

"The feds are going through his financials now and were able to trace some initial payments from a fake LLC that Powers had set up just for this purpose. It's going to take time, but they'll nail him."

"It's really over." The shake-up at the research institute had caused a lot of problems for her and the other professors who had not been involved. The dean of the Milwaukee College of Medicine was stepping in and had hired an auditing firm to go through all their financials. Roger Cannon wasn't involved, but he had announced his retirement, effective immediately. The lab was still being repaired, and as such, her research had come to a screeching halt.

It bothered her to know that Powers had gotten away with disrupting things as much as he had. But there was nothing she could do but to move forward from here. To keep plugging away until she was able to fulfill her mission to cure diabetes.

Funny thing was, though, the forced vacation had made her realize how much she'd missed. Over the past few weeks, Grayson had taken her swimming at Bradford Beach, to a concert on the Summerfest grounds, along with sampling several of his favorite restaurants. He'd also attended church with her and had taken her out on several double dates with his teammates and their wives.

She'd never had so much fun in her life. And while she wasn't giving up on her research by any stretch of the imagination, she now appreciated the importance of having balance in her life. God first, then Grayson, and then her research.

"I'm so happy," she said as Grayson grinned down at her. "I wasn't really afraid he'd come after me, but it's still a relief to have him behind bars.

"For both of us," Grayson admitted. He kissed her, and she knew she'd never get tired of his kisses. Then he finally set her on her feet. "Let's take a walk along the parkway."

Walking the parkway in the afternoon was their new favorite pastime. Her house was located on Maple Creek Parkway, a nice stretch of parkland where they often saw wildlife, deer, foxes, and even the occasional coyote. Summer was short in Wisconsin as Grayson always said, so they needed to enjoy it.

"Fine with me. Just let me save my work." It wasn't always easy to walk away from her research, but Grayson's good mood was infectious.

The summer sun was high in the sky. Grayson caught her hand as they strolled along the parkway. The scent of freshly cut grass and wildflowers filled the air. They didn't hurry, but Grayson tugged her to a stop when they reached their favorite set of trees. This was where they'd glimpsed the fox, but there was no sign of her now.

"Eve." He held her gaze for a moment, then slowly went down on one knee. She gasped when he pulled a small velvet ring box from his pocket and opened it. "Would you please marry me?"

"I—uh, it's only been three weeks!" It was too soon, wasn't it?

"I know, but we've known each other longer than that." He didn't move, even though they were getting curious looks from other pedestrians enjoying the summer day. "I love you. Please marry me."

"Yes, Grayson." No amount of time would change her love for him. She laughed as he slipped the ring onto her finger. "I can't wait to be your wife."

"Thank you for making me the happiest guy on earth." He rose to his feet, and a few people behind them clapped and whistled.

One even shouted, "You go, buddy! Grab the girl and kiss her!"

Laughing, Grayson drew her in for a kiss, then shouted, "She said yes!"

"Whoo-hoo!" someone shouted. "Congrats!"

She couldn't help but laugh too. She'd never been so happy. And she had God to thank for bringing them together.

I HOPE you enjoyed Grayson and Eve's story! It's been so much fun writing about the members of Rhy's tactical team. Are you ready to learn what Roscoe is up to? To read *Roscoe*, Click Here!

Thanks so much for reading my Oath of Honor series. I'm truly blessed to have wonderful readers like you. I hope you enjoyed Grayson and Eve's story. I've been having so much fun bringing the Finnegans and even the Callahans back into these books. What better way to keep track of what the family is up to.

Don't forget, you can purchase eBooks or audiobooks directly from my website, and you will receive a 15% discount by using the code **LauraScott15**.

I adore hearing from my readers! I can be found through my website at https://www.laurascottbooks.com, via Facebook at https://www.facebook.com/LauraScott Books, and Instagram at https://www.instagram.com/lauras cottbooks/. Please take a moment to subscribe to my YouTube channel at youtube.com/@LauraScottBooks-wr1xl?sub_confirmation=1, where you can listen to my audiobooks for free. Also, take a moment to sign up for my monthly newsletter to learn about my new book releases! All subscribers receive a free novella not available for purchase on any platform plus a bonus epilogue of Elly and Joe's wedding!

Until next time,

Laura Scott

PS: Read on for a sneak peek of *Roscoe*.

ROSCOE

Chapter One

Libby Hall gripped the steering wheel tightly, feeling certain the black truck two car lengths behind her was following her. Had been since she'd left the fleabag motel outside of Bloomington, Illinois.

Swallowing hard, she took note of the sign. Milwaukee, Wisconsin, was only ten miles away. Ten long miles until she reached Roscoe Turner. She took a deep breath and glanced down at her pregnant belly. "Soon, little one. We'll be safe soon."

Or so she hoped. Maybe she should have called Roscoe, rather than making the long and impulsive drive from Texas. But finding her apartment ransacked with a huge knife stuck in the middle of her kitchen table had rattled her.

Badly.

Roscoe had mentioned his cousin Cameron who lived in Milwaukee. She'd known Roscoe had left Texas after their huge fight; he was the one who helped arrest her brother in the first place. Using her to get to Tony. It had hurt that Roscoe had kept his role as a cop secret. Especially after they spent the night together.

Now here she was, tracking down his cousin, hoping Cameron would tell her where to find Roscoe.

She tried not to think about how she'd cried on Roscoe's shoulder after getting the news her father had died of a heart attack. How she'd spent the night with him, only to discover almost a week later that her brother Tony had been arrested thanks to Roscoe using her to get badly needed information to put her brother away for the rest of his life. Yes, her brother was a criminal, she didn't condone that behavior. At least Tony had cooperated with the DEA to give up the cartel.

Glancing in the rearview mirror and seeing that the black truck was still two cars back, she realized the cartel must have been involved in ransacking her apartment. That maybe they'd come after her out of revenge. Sending a loud message to anyone else who dared to testify against them.

Please, Lord, keep us safe in Your care!

This was Roscoe's fault.

No, that wasn't fair. Her brother Tony had been the one to transport drugs across the border. He'd done this. All Roscoe had done was to try to put a stop to it. And she couldn't blame him for that.

She could blame him for the way he'd gone about it. Making her believe he cared about her.

Letting her fall in love with him.

She carefully switched lanes, noting with a nauseating feeling of despair that the black truck followed suit. Glancing at her map app on her phone, she noted her exit was coming up. She waited until the last possible minute to get off the interstate, hoping the black truck would keep going. She turned right at the end of the ramp, then stomped on the gas to pick up speed.

The black truck was no longer behind her. Had she lost him?

She made another quick turn, then searched the street addresses. It helped that Cameron Stevenson's place wasn't too far from the interstate. She drove past the Wisconsin State Fair grounds, then turned left at the next cross street.

She pulled into the driveway, taking note of the squad sitting a few yards ahead of her. Was Cameron a cop too? Or was Roscoe here? She prayed it was the latter as she quickly slid out from behind the wheel, grabbed her purse, and hurried to the front door.

Leaning on the doorbell, she cast a furtive glance behind her. So far, the street was clear.

It seemed to take an inordinate length of time for the front door to open. Her eyes widened when she saw Roscoe standing there.

"Libby?" He looked confused, then his gaze dropped to her pregnant belly. His eyes bulged with shock. "What in the—you'll are *pregnant?*"

"Surprise." She winced at her snarky tone. "But worse, I'm in danger. Someone wrecked my apartment, leaving a large knife embedded in my table. I'm afraid the cartel is responsible." Now that she was there, she was hit by an overwhelming feeling of relief. "I came here because I need your help . . ."

His gaze narrowed on something behind her. She turned in time to see the black truck rolling down the street, the passenger window open, revealing a dark-skinned man. Certain the vehicle was the same one that had followed her from the Wisconsin/Illinois border, she instinctively ducked and darted away from the door just as the guy opened fire.

"Libby!" Roscoe flung the door open and stepped out holding his weapon with one hand. He fired at the retreating truck. She heard the metallic ping of the bullet striking the vehicle. Lifting her head, she saw the truck was still moving, but faster now as the driver tried to evade them.

"Get inside!" Roscoe leaned down and grabbed her arm. She didn't need to be told twice. She stumbled into the house, shivering despite the warm July sun. Roscoe was dressed in casual clothes, jeans and a T-shirt, which made her think he had the day off. But if that was the case, why was the squad in the driveway? "Who was that? What's going on?" he demanded.

"I—don't know." Tears pricked her eyes, and she tried to pull herself together. "I think that truck has been following me since I left the motel."

"What motel?" Roscoe stared at her, then waved his hand. "Never mind. We need to get you out of here before they come back for a second round."

"First, I have to use the bathroom." The baby had been sitting on her bladder for the last twenty miles.

He looked like he might argue, then waved toward the hallway. "Go ahead, but hurry. I'll call this in."

She hurried down the hall, listening as he made the call to report gunfire at this address. She was relieved to find Roscoe here, although she wasn't sure where Cameron was. Did the two guys share the house?

She told herself it didn't matter. She was here because Roscoe had started this nightmare by arresting her brother. By making the cartel angry enough to lash out at her.

Despite how much she detested what Roscoe had done,

using her to get to her brother, she needed him to keep her and their baby safe.

It was the least he could do.

———

LIBBY HALL WAS *pregnant with his child. And someone had just tried to kill her.*

Roscoe filled the local law enforcement in on the recent shooting. Then he called his boss, Captain Rhyland Finnegan of the Milwaukee Police Department Tactical Team. "I need a couple of days off."

"Okay," Rhy said after a long moment. "What's going on?"

He sighed, running his hand through his thick hair. "An old friend of mine showed up at the house, and someone tried to kill her."

"Did you call it in?" Rhy asked.

"Of course. But we can't stay here. I need to get her someplace safe." He was still reeling over Libby's unexpected arrival. "She's pregnant."

"Yours?"

"Yeah." He could take a paternity test, but the timing was right. Besides, Libby wasn't the type to sleep around. They—he shouldn't have taken advantage of her that night she'd learned her father had died. "I'm more concerned with keeping her safe."

"Understood. You can try heading to the American Lodge, but it may be booked this close to the Fourth of July. You may need to go farther out to find a room."

He hadn't considered the timing related to the holiday. He sighed. "Good point. In the meantime, I hope you don't hold this time off against me."

"You know me better than that," Rhy chided. "Family first."

Family. The word was like a sucker punch to the gut. Roscoe's cousin Cameron was the only family he had left after losing his adoptive parents. And while he and Cam were close now, they hadn't met until they were teenagers because their mothers were estranged. He liked Cam but was keenly aware that there was no blood bond between them.

Libby's baby proved he had a family now. No matter how things worked out for him and Libby, he would not abandon his child.

"Thanks, Rhy." He lowered the phone as Libby emerged from the bathroom. She looked as beautiful as always, despite the fear darkening her green eyes. Before he could say anything more, the wail of sirens filled the air. He raised his voice to be heard over the noise. "Please sit down and wait here. I need to talk to these officers before we head out."

She nodded, sinking into the closest chair and clutching her purse like a lifeline. He had so many questions, but right now, he needed to stay focused on finding those gunmen.

He strode to the door and watched as two local squads pulled up. Glancing back at Libby, he offered a reassuring smile as he headed outside to meet them.

"Officer Roscoe Turner from MPD," he said, showing his badge. "An extended cab Chevy truck drove past and fired two rounds at my—ah, Libby Hall." He'd stumbled over how to introduce Libby. She wasn't exactly his girlfriend any longer, although they had been close.

Until she'd learned he'd arrested her brother Tony for running drugs.

"License plate?" Officer Golden asked.

"No, it was partially covered in mud." Not to mention the whole thing had gone down too fast for him to get more than a passing glimpse. He turned to look at Cameron's house. "Here"—he pointed to the small round bullet holes in the siding—"these are the two slugs."

"We'll get them out and examined for markings," the second officer by the name of Avery replied.

The slugs were in the exact location Libby had been standing before she'd ducked to avoid them. The near miss made his blood run cold.

"We'd like to speak to Ms. Hall," Golden said.

"Sure." He led the way inside where Libby was still seated on the sofa. Seeing them, she struggled to her feet. He quickly crossed over to offer a hand. "Libby, Officer Golden and Officer Avery would like to ask you a few questions."

She looked at the cops warily. "I'm not sure I can be much help. I noticed the black truck keeping pace behind me after I left my motel earlier this morning. I—uh, came to Wisconsin to find Roscoe—er, Officer Turner. I—uh . . ." She floundered for a moment, then said, "My brother Tony Hall is in a federal prison for drug trafficking. He had once been working with some faction of the Mexican cartel."

Golden whistled. "I wouldn't want to mess with the cartels."

The color drained from Libby's face. "I was told Tony cooperated with the DEA for a lighter sentence. He's been in prison for about six months, but two days ago, when I came home from work, I found my apartment totally ransacked, and worse, a large knife was sticking out of the kitchen table." She bit her lower lip for a moment, pulling herself together before continuing. "I'm a teacher. I knew this had to be related to my brother. Fearing for my life and that of my child, I jumped in the car and drove away."

Roscoe felt sick knowing that arresting Tony had put Libby and their baby in danger. Worse, she'd had her apartment trashed, then had been forced to drive for two days straight to get here. He should have stayed in Texas.

He should have been there for her all this time.

The two officers glanced at each other with concern. Golden asked, "You believe one of the Mexican cartels has followed you all the way here?"

"It's the only thing that makes sense." Libby sniffed and swiped at her damp eyes. "But I didn't notice anyone following me until I reached the Wisconsin state line." She shivered despite the warmth. "I guess I could have missed a tail after leaving Texas, but I was paying attention. Especially knowing someone had left a knife in my apartment." She swallowed hard and glanced at him. "I'm glad you were here. If you hadn't answered the door . . ."

"I'm glad I was here too." He ached to take her into his arms but couldn't seem to bring himself to close the gap between them. She had only sought him out now because of the danger.

Not because she was desperate to see him. In fact, he wasn't sure he'd have learned about the baby if her apartment hadn't been broken in to.

His stomach tightened with anger and frustration with both the situation and his own role in it. What had happened back in Texas? Was Tony still alive? In his experience, snitches were often killed in prison. But it also wasn't unheard of to kill the snitch's family as punishment for ratting out the cartel. Which was why getting anyone to testify against them was difficult.

He turned toward Golden. "I need to get Ms. Hall out

of here and somewhere safe. I've contacted my boss, Captain Rhy Finnegan, to let him know about the shooting. He may want to work with your captain about getting results from the evidence collection." He snapped his fingers. "I almost forgot. I returned fire and struck the truck. I don't think the bullet did much damage, though, because they sped out of here without stopping."

"We can be on the lookout for a black truck sporting a bullet hole," Avery said.

He nodded, even though he suspected the shooters would have ditched the truck by now and picked up something else.

At least, that's what he would have done.

"I think we may need to get the DEA here involved too," Golden said with a frown. "If the cartel is here, they'll need to know."

"Yeah, okay." He should have thought of that for himself. Roscoe doubted the DEA knew anything about the break-in back in Texas, though. "You can let the DEA here know that I worked with a DEA agent by the name of Charlie Olson down south. They should collaborate on this." In his humble opinion, the more law enforcement officers involved, the better. "I'd be happy to talk to the DEA representative here in Milwaukee once I have Ms. Hall safe."

"Good idea." Golden took a step back and lifted his hand to his radio.

Roscoe turned toward Libby. She looked pale and exhausted. Traumatized by finding her place broken in to, threatened with a knife, then being followed and shot at. Not to mention traveling across the entire country. "Can you give me a few more minutes to grab some gear? Then we'll hit the road."

She nodded and sank back down onto the edge of the sofa. He ran to his guest bedroom and tossed some things into a duffel bag. Then he called Cameron, who was out of town for the week visiting his girlfriend in Madison. His cousin didn't answer, so he left a message instructing him to stay away from the house until they talked.

Hoping Cameron would call him back sooner rather than later, he joined Libby in the living room. Officer Golden crossed toward him. "I need your contact information. And Ms. Hall's too. I've been told that a DEA agent by the name of Doug Bridges wants to chat with both of you."

"Fine." He quickly rattled off his cell phone. "There's no point in taking down Ms. Hall's number, we're not keeping that phone."

"Oh, yeah. That makes sense." Golden frowned. "How will he get in touch with her?"

"Through me." He caught Libby's startled gaze. "I'm sorry, Libby, but we don't know how these guys tracked you. We can't risk you keeping that phone."

"I understand." She dug in her purse, then held it out to him. "Take it. I don't want those men to find me again."

He did so, powered it down, then stomped on it with his foot, grinding his heel into the device until it was destroyed. Then he picked up the pieces and tossed them into the garbage. Returning to Libby's side, he held out his hand to help her up. "Let's go."

"I have a suitcase in my car," Libby said.

He hesitated, then nodded, realizing she needed proper maternity clothes. The fact that she was pregnant with their child was still a shocker. Yet he couldn't allow that to sidetrack him. There would be time to discuss that more later.

Once they were safe.

He slung the duffel over his shoulder and grabbed the

keys to the squad. The good news was that his truck was at the precinct where there was no way the gunmen could have seen it.

"Stay behind me," he said in a low voice. "We'll get your suitcase, then climb into the squad."

She nodded without saying anything. Her wide eyes spoke volumes as he pushed open the front door and stepped out onto the porch. He scanned the surrounding neighborhood but didn't see anything alarming.

As promised, Libby hung back, allowing him to lead the way. When he stopped at the trunk of her car, she bumped into him.

"Sorry." She sounded embarrassed. Then she clicked the key fob to open the trunk. Her suitcase was small and looked brand new. It gave him pause.

He glanced at her over his shoulder. "Did you buy this along the way?"

"Yes. I drove without stopping until Oklahoma, then stopped in Illinois to buy the suitcase, prenatal vitamins, and a change of clothes. Why?"

"Cash or credit?" Even as he asked, he knew.

"Credit. I don't carry that much cash around." Realization dawned. "They tracked my credit card?"

"Possibly." Although he wondered why they hadn't picked her up at one of the gas stations along the way. Maybe she had already reached Illinois by the time they had gotten hold of her credit card information.

He lifted her pink suitcase out of the back and carried it to the squad. He set it down to open the passenger door for her. Moments later, he was backing down the driveway, keeping a wary eye out for the black truck.

There was a long silence before she spoke. "I guess you're wondering about the baby."

"Yeah, although I'm mostly wondering why you didn't reach out to me as soon as you found out the news." He cast a sidelong glance at her. "I would have come back to Texas."

She grimaced. "I didn't want you to be a part of my baby's life."

That casual comment was like a donkey kick to the chest. "What do you mean? I'm the baby's father, aren't I?"

"Yes. But you only pretended to care about me to get to my brother." She averted her gaze, staring out the window. "You really hurt me, Roscoe."

"I'm sorry." He tried to think of a way to reassure her. "I wasn't dating you only to get to your brother. I cared about you, Libby."

"Yeah, sure." She shook her head, and his stomach twisted when he saw the glint of tears in her eyes. "I don't believe you. Just drop it, okay? That doesn't matter now. It's your fault I'm in danger in the first place."

His fault? He grimaced, following her logic. "Because I arrested Tony."

"Yes." She sighed. "I understand you had a job to do and that my brother was mixed up in a dangerous crowd. I know that. But somehow, I'm the one with a target on my back."

That was all true. But if anyone else had arrested Tony, she would be in the same situation.

His gaze dropped to her belly, then darted back to the road. Almost the same situation, he silently amended. Maybe if he hadn't arrested Tony, he and Libby would still be together.

"I'm sorry you're in this situation. If I had known you would be in danger, I wouldn't have left. I was under the impression that Tony would be moved to a prison out of state and the cartel would never know who had given them up."

She shrugged but still didn't meet his gaze. "Whatever."

Maybe she had a reason to be angry with him. He had gotten to know her because she was Tony's sister. But his feelings for her had been real. He'd been attracted to her the first time he saw her, checking groceries at the store, a part-time job she held during the summers and over some weekends. He would have dated her no matter what his job entailed.

Yet he also knew their night together shouldn't have happened. She'd been reeling from her father's heart attack, and he'd allowed things go too far.

A week after he'd arrested Tony, she'd told him to get lost and never come back. He'd foolishly taken her at her word. His boss had told him that he should get out of the state for a while, until everything had settled down with the drug cartel. He'd heard about the opening on the tactical team from his cousin, Cam, and had applied, never expecting to get the job.

Thankfully, Rhy had hired him, and he was just starting to feel like a member of the team, rather than the outsider.

Yet he knew he'd give up his role on the team and more to support Libby and their child.

He pulled his wayward thoughts together with an effort. This wasn't the time to be dreaming of what his future might look like. They needed to find the gunmen and uncover who had sent them chasing her over several state lines.

The more he thought about Libby being followed all the way from Texas, the more he realized this never should have happened.

Was there a leak inside the prison system? One of the guards or maybe an inside informant?

Or was the leak within law enforcement, either the border patrol or the DEA?

He was about to call Rhy to let him know his concerns when he saw a large black truck coming up fast on his tail.

"Hang on," he warned, punching the gas and cranking on the wheel.

"Roscoe!" Libby grabbed the hand rest, clinging onto it for dear life. "The truck is back?"

He took a sharp right-hand turn, then hit the gas again to put more distance between them. He flipped on the overhead lights and sirens to force everyone around him to get out of the way.

A crack of gunfire followed by the shattering of the back window of the squad only made things worse. He had a clear path ahead of him, but so did the truck.

He managed to key his radio. "Unit fourteen requesting backup! Taking gunfire from a black Chevy truck!"

"Roger that, unit fourteen. What's your twenty?"

He didn't have time to respond when another crack of gunfire echoed from behind him. Roscoe wrenched the wheel to the left and headed toward the precinct.

Praying they'd get there before another round disabled the squad, leaving them as sitting ducks with nowhere to hide.

www.ingramcontent.com/pod-product-compliance
Lightning Source LLC
Chambersburg PA
CBHW070416310726
48977CB00003B/720